SWORDS OF TALERA

SWORDS OF TALERA

BEING

THE FIRST BOOK OF
THE TALERA CYCLE

by

Charles Allen Gramlich

The Borgo Press
An Imprint of Wildside Press

MMVII

CONTENTS

To My Mother

Anna Bell

INTRODUCTION

There is a man I know whose name is Ruenn Maclang. I first met him in October of 1987, on a Saturday evening when rain lashed cold against my windows and lightning forked the sky. I was working—or trying to work—on some financial reports for the university where I sometimes taught. The knock that rang loud on my door around 5:30 that evening made a welcome distraction.

I did not, at the time, know the man who stood on my porch. I still know very little about him. I remember that he was taller than I, a bit over six feet, with broad shoulders and dark brown hair cut rather long. His eyes were green, set deep behind sharp, almost harsh features. A thin scar, light against his deeply tanned skin, traced the angle of his left jaw, enhancing that harshness. He was not handsome but neither would he be overlooked in a crowd. There was about him a raw vitality that drew one's glance, an energy that crackled like heat lightning in his smoldering gaze.

He shook my hand as he introduced himself. His grip was dry, despite the rain, and full of latent power that he chose not to exert. Though somewhat ill at ease in his presence, I invited him in when he made it clear that he had business to discuss. He accepted the beer I offered and sipped it slowly while I added more wood to the fire to combat a chill that had entered through the open door. Though his clothes—jeans, cotton shirt, and an old overcoat—were soaked, my guest did not seem bothered by the cold and did not shiver.

As I finished stoking the fire and laid aside the poker, Ruenn Maclang put down his beer. "I have need of your services," he said.

His voice was low, his words oddly inflected and some-how archaic sounding to my ears.

"You're looking for financial advice?" I asked.

"Yes."

"Couldn't it have waited until Monday?"

"I did not wish to come to your office."

"Why not?"

He did not speak but reached inside his coat and re-moved a portion of the lining. He then lifted out two leather pouches tied with yellow cord and, leaning over, spilled the contents of the larger pouch onto my floor. I caught a wink of light reflected from the fire and gasped. A fortune in jew-els had just been poured onto my carpet. Sapphires flashed blue amid diamonds of ice and emeralds of dark green. A topaz gleamed yellow against rose opals, and strings of pale pearls lay draped softly and seductively across the harder stones.

There were other gems as well, in saffron and cinnabar and a dozen other exotic colors whose names I did not know, and there were tiny figurines of what I thought were mythi-cal beasts, carved in jade, and ivory, and onyx. I reached down and plucked up a blood ruby. It caught the firelight and burst into dazzling cold flame in my hand.

I looked up at Ruenn Maclang. Was he a thief, I won-dered? He sensed my thoughts, or read them in my face.

"They are not stolen," he said. "They are mine to do with as I wish."

I only nodded.

"I am," he continued, "often out of the country and un-able to conduct my affairs here. I need an agent to carry out certain tasks for me, such as the exchange of these stones and the investment of what money they bring. Also, there are places where I would like money to be sent. I assure you it is nothing illegal and you will be well paid."

To punctuate his words he tossed me the smaller of the two leather pouches he had taken from his coat. I caught it, hearing the chink of metal on metal. I untied the thong bind-ing and spilled five coins into my hand. In the firelight they gleamed the rich, butter yellow of gold. A man's hawk-like face filled the front of the coins and on the reverse soared a large bird of prey, talons extended. I recognized neither the bird nor the man.

A distinctive mint mark, like a broken dagger, shone beneath the bird's left claw. I had seen coins much like these before, but only in museums. Each piece varied slightly, indicating that they had been struck by hand rather than by machine, and the last such coins were probably minted on Earth several hundred years ago. Yet, these were shiny and unworn, as if new.

"These must be worth a considerable sum of money," I said.

"Here, perhaps," Maclang replied.

I did not understand what he meant.

"Why come to me?" I asked. "I know nothing of jewels or ancient coins."

He grinned, making his face suddenly less harsh. "Well, I know few people here, and I thought that since we were cousins you might help me."

I was startled. "I didn't know there were any Maclangs in my family."

"Not many," he admitted, shrugging.

"So how are we related?"

He smiled mysteriously. "It *is* somewhat distant." Then he became serious. "I must be leaving. Will you help me?"

To my surprise, I found myself agreeing, not for the gold but for something I saw or sensed in the character of Ruenn Maclang.

"I need to know exactly what you want me to do," I told him.

"The full instructions are in here," he said, handing me a vellum folder. "Most concern the funds I wish to have distributed."

I opened the folder and quickly scanned the sheaf of papers inside. "It may be difficult," I told him.

"Use whatever money you need," he said, waving a hand at the jewels. "From time to time I may return to see how things have gone. I will probably want access to currency but I can bring more gems and gold as they are required."

"I assume you wish to be discrete?"

"If at all possible, Charles. I will trust your judgment."

I accepted his trust and it is for such reasons that I cannot reveal to you the fullness of Ruenn's instructions to me concerning the disposition of the money I acquired from the jewels.

Maclang rose to go, holding out his hand. I took it, feeling again the reserved power in that grip.

"Thank you," he said.

"You're welcome."

He hesitated for a moment at the door and then, as if it were an afterthought, reached into his coat and drew out a manuscript wrapped in soft brown leather. You now hold that manuscript in your hands.

"By the way," he said, facing me, "I have something else here that you might find of interest. It is a book of adventures." He smiled. "Fiction, of course."

Of course. But while he spoke I studied him. His smile was slight and his eyes looked far away.

"I know you have written a few things yourself in a similar vein," he went on. "I fear this is not very good, but if you think it publishable you may keep half of whatever it makes." He laid the manuscript on a table, turned, and went out.

I followed him to the door but he had already disappeared. I heard no car engine start and wondered if he had walked, though I live far out of town. The rain had stopped and a few stars peeked through the scattering clouds. My breath smoked in the growing cold. I returned to the warmth of my home, hoping that Maclang did not have far to go. Strangely, I had the feeling that he had very far to go indeed.

Much later that night, I finally unwrapped the manuscript and sat down to read. The words had been written in dark ink on thin sheets of rough brown paper. The hand was bold and scrawling. I remember dimly the clock striking eleven when I began, but I recall little else that went on around me until dawn broke. Only then did I put down the story, because I was finished.

I sat there for a moment with the strange, alien scent of the manuscript pages still on my fingers, and closed my eyes to envision what I had read. Could Ruenn Maclang really have possessed such a fierce imagination? It is either that or he has been to the planet he calls Talera, which is far distant from Earth—been there, and fought there, and won a place. But, of course, that is absurd. Yet, I remember that faraway cool look in his eyes when he spoke of his writings, and there are things I have discovered since his visit that have only deepened the mystery.

There was indeed a Ruenn Maclang in my mother's family tree. He and his brother Bryce disappeared off the coast of Japan in 1914. As far as I have been able to ascertain, no one else by that name has been born since. Then there are the gold coins that he gave me. There are no traces of them to be found in Earth's past, no city or empire that can be shown to have minted them. They are unique and untraceable.

But, perhaps Ruenn Maclang will return someday, as he hinted that he might. I have many questions to ask if he does. Until then, I'll let you read his story. Make of it what you will.

—Charles Allen Gramlich

CHAPTER ONE

TRANSIT

The snow falls outside my window, painting the evening world in white, and I can hear the cold wind against the shutters searching for a way to come in. A fire leaps in the hearth against the encroaching chill but I feel little need of its heat. There are memories to warm me. As I put down these words those memories return as if the events of months ago had only just happened. I do not know what compels me to record those hours, those days. Perhaps it is simply that I would hold onto the memories before they grow old.

I was born in California, in the United States of America, in 1888. My parents were Kendall Maclang, who ran a small shipping enterprise out of San Francisco, and Cathlin Ryall Maclang, whose family owned a vineyard in the Sacramento Valley. I have a younger brother named Bryce, and two sisters: Andrea, who is the oldest of us, and Elisabeth, who is called after her grandmother and is the youngest of all. I was named Ruenn. I do not know why for it is an odd name—descended from the Irish Ruane—but my very Irish mother liked it and my Scottish father could deny her nothing. I do not mind, having become accustomed to it.

In 1904 I accompanied my father on a trip to Japan that saw the beginning of a profitable trade with that country. Maclang ships hauled timber and ore west to the islands of the sun and returned laden with silks and spices and the finely crafted loveliness of an ancient land. I remember well one such work of art, given to my father on that first voyage as a seal for our bargain with the Japanese. This was the *dai-*

sho, the twin swords carried by the ancient, but not yet extinct, warrior caste of Japan.

I mention the blades here because their like play a role in this story, though when I first saw them I did not think of the sword's long association with death and war. To me they were the distilled essence of beauty. I know now that it is a poisoned beauty, albeit not without its power to turn men's minds.

Still, I am grateful for that gift of long ago. Without it I would never have taken up the sword and learned its demands, and that knowledge has preserved my life, and that of those I love, more than once. The Japanese still treasure the sword and the art of its use, and for some reason there were those among my father's friends who took a liking to me and taught me their martial skills.

Just as the sword has played a part in my life, so too has the sea, and for a much longer time. I grew up around the ocean and around ships, and captained my first voyage to Japan at age twenty. I have captained such voyages many times since. The sea often took me away from home—so often that it came to seem like home after a while—but I did not have to grow to love it. I loved it from the moment I saw it.

In the early autumn of 1914, while war raged in Europe, my brother accompanied me on the long journey to Japan. He was nineteen to my twenty-six. Rumors abounded that the United States might enter the conflict against the Central Powers. If it came to that then both Bryce and I would enlist, but I was not sure Bryce would wait that long. He was headstrong and impatient, and thought more often of war's glory than of war's pain. Though not wishing it, my parents would not have forbidden Bryce to enlist. Instead, they sent him to Japan with me and hoped the trip would take his mind off it.

"He is too young," my father told me just before we left port.

I grinned. "If his hair were gray he'd still be too young," I said.

"Yes," my father replied seriously. "One's sons are always too young to go to war."

We left San Francisco in mid-September. It was not the

14

most propitious time to cross the North Pacific but it had been a good year for trade and we hoped to complete one more voyage before winter set in. On the Twentieth of September, 1914, Bryce and I went ashore on a tiny island off the coast of Japan and disappeared from the face of the Earth.

These facts should have been recorded because many of the ship's crew did not disappear with us. Perhaps such records could be found, or there may be those still living who recall the mystery. If so, you will have to find them. I am in no position to do so.

There was nothing particularly unusual about our reasons for going ashore on that island. We had ridden out a gale during the night that wrenched plates at our bow and allowed water to seep through the strained seams. The damage was slight but the forward cargo hold had partially flooded.

Toward midmorning, with the last of the storm froth slipping behind us, we passed an island to starboard and anchored there to make some repairs and replenish our water supply, which had grown low. A lushness of tangled plants and vines promised more than one freshwater spring, and to the east of the cove where we anchored a cataract spread mist on the air that drew rainbows in the sunshine. The sky in the wake of the storm was clear and bright, and very blue.

Bryce went ashore with a dozen men and they returned with brimming casks of sweet water and armfuls of fresh fruit to make a welcome addition to our rations. The repair of the ship was not so easily accomplished. It took hours of struggling knee deep in greasy bilge water before we managed to seal off the leaks and pump the hold dry. Final repairs could wait until we made port.

In the fading afternoon light, I allowed the crew ashore and most took the opportunity to bathe in the silken stillness of the cove. I scrubbed away my own coat of grime and later strolled along the beach with Bryce and our cousin Eric Ryall, who had joined the family business. It was a peaceful evening.

The men were weary from battling the storm and I gave in when they asked to spend the night at anchor. But I too

15

wished it. Eric and a few others even asked to sleep ashore, and I agreed. There seemed little danger. Perhaps I should not have allowed it, but it was my decision, and should I have it to make again, with no more knowledge than I possessed at that time, the decision would be the same.

Looking back now on that evening, I remember only one portent of the strangeness to come. Near twilight the birds fell silent in the trees and vast flocks of them rose and flew to the west. I thought little of it at the time. The day had been long and I was pleasantly tired. With the ship rocking gently beneath me, I went early to bed and quickly entered a sound sleep.

Well after dark I awoke, an unidentifiable fear prickling coldly at my neck. I lay still for a moment, listening to the night sounds of the ship. There was nothing unusual among them. Yet the thought, the sensation that something was wrong, did not go away. I pushed back the covers and sat up.

A scream ripped high and shrill across the darkness, rising from the shore where my men slept. I rushed madly up the stairs onto the deck only to find the beach where the camp lay pervaded by a pulsing green haze. The center of that haze was a writhing mass of shadows. A bass throbbing rose and fell with each pulse of emerald light, and over the vibration lay the screams of my men, crawling up the scale until their voices teetered on the edge of soundlessness. Then the screams were gone and the cold, verdant fire went with them.

The watch and I stood in stunned horror as other crewmen staggered from below to join us. Several men crossed themselves. Others fell to their knees with muttered prayers.

"Ghost lights," one man stated under his breath.

"Belay that!" I snapped. "Those are no ghosts."

I turned to the others, my brother among them. "I'm going ashore," I told them. "Bryce, get the pistols from my cabin. I'll need five men with guns. See to it."

He hurried off.

Burke Tompkins was my first officer, and a good one. Without waiting to hear the order, he ran off to fetch some lanterns and prepare one of the ship's boats.

I spoke to the remaining crewmen. "I don't know what's

happened, but there must be a natural explanation. We'll find it. Mr. Tompkins is in charge until I return. If we're not back by dawn then send a larger party in search. Make sure they're armed but be careful. It won't help if we start shooting each other."

I then turned and hurried to the rail where one of the ship's boats was being lowered over the side. Bryce joined me, handing over a Colt revolver and retaining another for himself. With him were several other crewmen, their weapons glinting dully in the lantern light. Seven of us pushed away from the ship, and working our oars together we swiftly brought the boat to shore.

Barely a quarter of an hour had passed since we'd heard the first screams, but the beach lay empty of life. There *were* signs of a struggle. Coals from the fire lay scattered wildly about, many still gleaming red. The tents and sleeping bags were torn and mauled, the earth trampled. A coffee pot had been crushed flat as if stomped on by a giant. What in heaven's name had happened here? And where were my men? There was no blood so I could hope that they lived. But where were they?

I looked up at the ebon hills above us, searching for an answer to my question. And it came. Within the darkness, as if waiting for my glance, a single point of emerald flame burst into unholy life. A second joined it, and a third, and more, until dozens of torches danced together like a rose of fire. I checked the loads in my pistol, feeling the hairs at the nape of my neck rise and stir with a life of their own. There was something too much like a lure in those lights.

"Whot the 'ell's going on 'ere," a stocky crewman named McCollum said. It was not a question.

"Don't know," I replied anyway. "But whoever is playing with those lights knows, and we're going to find out. Let's go."

I started up toward the hills, toward a dim trail faintly silvered by the newly risen moon, and in my head I thought: *whoever or whatever*. But I did not say it.

The trail grew steeper as we climbed, and treacherous with loose stones. We had gone halfway up to where the first torches flickered when we came to a wide place in the path and stopped to catch a breath. As we stood there, the wind shifted toward us, bringing a scent of honeysuckle and a sound like chimes ringing in an old hollow barrel. When the sound touched us, the lights winked out. The music and wind faded, too, but slowly, lingeringly.

The moon had been captured by clouds and the darkness above us seemed absolute after the brighter moments before. With our own lanterns providing the only light now, we started once more up the path and did not stop until we reached the crest of the hill. The wind found us again there, bringing the music with it, and as if summoned the lights flickered on a few hundred yards to our left. The torches burned stronger this time and we forced our way toward them through the beginnings of heavy brush. They receded before us, dancing frenziedly, always just ahead.

The lure of the lights strengthened, and the music and the honeysuckle scent drew cloyingly about us, urging us on with soft fingers. The night warmed. The voices of frogs and insects grew distant, and the trees cast ghostly green shadows as we passed on heavy feet beneath their clawing limbs.

I stumbled over a root and sudden fear flushed my skin with sweat. Glancing about, I saw my men with slack faces, their hands loose on their weapons. They jumped and looked guilty as I snapped at them. Almost, we had fallen under the torches' spell. Almost, but not quite. As if angered, the lights winked out again.

The night grew long. The lights were near and then far, always out of reach. They beckoned us to follow and were gone when we arrived. At last, with the lights lost and the final stars fading, we came to a dead end. Sharp ravines fell away to either side, mist rivers running in their depths. At our feet a black cliff rose five hundred feet into the air. Broken talus beneath our boots attested to its instability. I reached for a handhold and found my fist full of crumbled stone.

"All right. What do we do now?" Bryce asked.

"Wait until morning," I said. "But not in here. I don't care for places with only one exit."

We turned to go and our shadows fell suddenly out before us, though it was not yet dawn. In unison we looked back and up. The cliff was crowned with a halo of green fire and the black stone below lay dappled with emerald. A small marble shrine was thrown into stark relief by the flames. That building seemed very fragile and open at first glance, and I wondered if we might not find answers there.

I glanced back to the cliff. Handholds, unseen in the darkness, were visible now, limned by flickering fire. I found one that bore my weight and started up the side. The men followed, cursing as sharp pebbles gouged their flesh. We moved by inches, our world filled only with the rhythm of moving hands and feet, and with green shadows. But slowly we crawled upward. I prayed the lights would not go out again. Their glow was all that stood between us and death from a missed step in the dark. At last, though, we bellied over the top of the cliff and drew a breath that wasn't full of rock dust.

The lights did not disappear as I expected but receded into the forest to form a rough semicircle about our party. From what I could see, nothing held them up. They danced in eldritch silence, five feet off the ground. In their midst lay the shrine we had seen from below. It no longer seemed fragile, only cold and white and bitter.

We approached the building carefully, weapons ready. Bryce and I went first up the steps, he because of his eager curiosity and I because I feared for my brother. In the nave of the temple, night shadows clustered thickly, their weight broken only by a silver gleam the color of old moonlight. On a black altar set in the middle of the stone floor lay a crystal gem the size of my fist. It pulsed with an argent light that formed a spherical envelope a dozen feet across around the altar. At the sphere's border, where light and dark met, eerie motes of golden shimmer swirled.

In the center of the jewel appeared a spot of pale gray, a pearl of ashes. As we watched that point it began to expand, swallowing the gem and the altar and stopping only when it was as large as the bed of a wagon standing upright. To look upon it was like looking into a gulf of madness.

The feeling stole across me that this was a door, a door into smoke and swirling mist. An instant later that feeling became conviction as a being stepped through the portal. The thing's body was human-like but it was not a man. Its flesh gleamed an iridescent green and gold; scales covered it like armor. A broad, thick tail stretched away into the gray fog behind it.

The creature's face was an abomination, calling up visions of fallen angels burning centuries in hell. The eyes shone flat and stone blue, without whites. Two slits gashed the face where the nose should have been and the mouth below glistened wide and red, lined with yellowed fangs. Large vanes, like the wings of bats, extended from either side of the beast's head, fluttering with each harsh breath it drew.

The creature held out a hand to us. The appendage seemed human enough, except for the scales, but I had no time to count whether it had a normal complement of digits. Clutched in the hand was a translucent wand about two feet long, and its tip began to gleam, bleeding emerald color off into the space around it.

The beast spoke. I did not understand its words but the sound of them sent fingers of nausea twisting through me. The words grew louder. They were not addressed to us but seemed an incantation of some sort. As if answering that profane chant, the radiance forming at the tip of the wand began to draw itself into long veins of cold fire that flowed viscously through the argent envelope around the altar.

Color began to gather against the side of the sphere nearest us and spread out over the surface like a ghastly fungus. It pulsed obscenely, eating away at the silver envelope of light. A sudden stench burned my nostrils and the first ringing alarms of terror clanged through my head. My heart pounded; my mouth went as dry as the morning after a bout of hard drinking.

At that moment, Bryce took a step forward and started to raise his pistol. When his arm was extended it would strike the light sphere at the exact point where the sickly green glow writhed most strongly. Suddenly ill with horror, I knew that if he touched that place he would bring destruction on us all.

With a shouted "No!" I leaped forward and grabbed my brother's shoulder just as the pistol barrel struck the envelope of light. Electricity crackled along the contact point and the gun exploded in Bryce's fist. He screamed in agony, and the beast within the sphere matched him as the discharging bullet shattered the wand it held and struck it in the chest.

In a frozen moment, I saw the creature raise its hands as if to ward itself and heard it shout a single word, "*Nethcormundis.*" Then the sun erupted out of the strange portal in which the being stood, turning it into a blazing pillar of light. The flame burst outward along the veins of emerald color and disintegrated the outer membrane of the envelope in a coruscation of rainbow embers. For an instant, Bryce and I were limned in green fire that clung like ice to our flesh. It must have been that which saved us from what followed.

The sun at the core of the sphere convulsed in its death throes. Even through the cold that surrounded us I felt the surge of heat that blistered past and turned the crewmen behind me into cinders where they stood. They did not scream, for there was no time, but we could not have heard them anyway as a crescendo of wind and flame raced all around us. The island trembled and staggered as if in pain. The stone itself began to melt and run.

But the outward explosion continued only a moment. More quickly than it had come, the crashing light imploded into the hole where the door had been. I lost my grip on Bryce's shoulder as we were sucked forward into a gaping maw of nothingness. The pistol spun from my fingers. In the roaring darkness, I screamed Bryce's name but could not even hear myself. The world went inside out. Pain tore at my flesh. Objects struck me and whirled away. A crushing chill held me for an instant and was gone, and I fell, as if from a great height.

I struck water and flailed my way to the surface. Salt stung like acid on my skin, as if my whole body was raw, but I ignored the hurt and yelled frantically for my brother. No answer came.

Knuckling half blind eyes until tears flowed, I managed to wash away enough of the darkness to find myself adrift like a piece of wood in a vast expanse of blue ocean. Short, choppy waves tossed briny water in my face. The sky overhead was dark and lowering, and so overcast that no hint of the sun peeked through.

Nowhere did I see the island from which I must have been thrown, and there was no sign of Bryce either. I struck out in search of him, diving again and again into the cool depths. But there was nothing. No debris. Nothing. Yet, I had felt his presence near me as we fell, even as we passed through the utter cold that made me think of death, and it was only an instant before I hit that he had slipped away into an alternate blackness.

Once more I dived. I went deep, and deeper, until my lungs were bursting and inky spots danced like dust motes before my eyes. But Bryce was not to be found. At last, I returned to the surface and clung there, numbed by shock and exhaustion. Consciousness began to slip away and I thought only that it would be easy to die here. My eyelids seemed to close by themselves.

Through the roaring in my ears I heard a sound like that made by a ship foaming through the water. My eyes opened, and there was indeed a ship bearing down upon me. Its hull was of wood that had been painted white, and vast yellow sails billowed in the wind. At the prow hung the likeness of some mythical beast that stood as tall as two men. Its neck was arched to strike and it might have been a cat except that it lacked ears and was covered with scales. Flags and pennons streamed from the ship's masts, snapping in a stiff breeze. They were yellow with a black border, and the image of the reptile/cat—also in black—was guardant in the center.

I had seen wooden ships before but never such a ship as this. It was, as one would say about horses, short coupled. Its primary motive power appeared to be sails, but a single deck of oar-ports ran along either side. The design seemed archaic but it moved with grace and power, and so swiftly did it come that I failed to realize for a moment that I was about to be run down.

There is something about approaching violent death that revitalizes flagging energies amazingly. Frantically, I began to wave my arms and found new voice with which to yell. The sailors aboard that ship had keen senses and saw me in time. There came a strange, high shout and the prow warped hard to port and passed me by. The ship slowed and tacked back into the wind as far as it could go, and a small boat was lowered over the side to race toward me.

I raised a weak hand, the remnants of my strength drained away by my latest exertions. I knew the boat must be coming closer but in my mind it seemed to recede, and the world with it. My vision reeled and darkened and the roaring in my ears grew louder. Seawater sloshed in my mouth, making me gag.

Suddenly, the boat was within reach. Faces peered over the side; strong arms reached down to grab me. I looked at the faces and thought I must be delirious.

Delirium gave way to insanity. Another face peered over the boat's coaming. It was small and bright eyed, with the features of a fox. A black stripe ran across its nose. The creature stood up on its hind feet and held something in its front paws, something very much like a reed pipe. It began to play, the melody haunting.

Quickly then, awareness left me.

CHAPTER TWO

ARRIVAL

I came to on the deck of the ship with cold seawater being dashed in my face. I knew the treatment, having used it myself to roust sailors out of their bunks after a long period ashore and too much ale.

I opened my eyes and the faces from my delirium were still there. They were human faces, though strangely formed, with jutting jaws and thick lips, and heavy lashes that hung over dark but laughing eyes. The bodies, too, were human, but dwarfish, with broad shoulders and barrel chests and short, squat trunks on bowed legs. Their arms were longer than a man's in proportion to their bodies and were knotted with muscle.

The tallest of the beings stood a little over five and a half feet, the shortest around four feet. All were dressed in cotton breeches and buff tunics. Their feet were bare and calloused. Circlets of gold clasped their arms and bright jewels flashed at their ears. Their trousers were sashed with yellow and red and blue, and the hilts of daggers and short swords protruded from behind the sashes.

It seemed I had awakened on a sailing ship of centuries ago, a ship crewed by dwarves and with a fox that walked on two feet and played the pipes for a mascot. Strange, I did not recall going on a drinking binge last night. I closed my eyes in hopes the dream would end and I would find myself back on my own ship. Another bucket of seawater plashed in my face.

Spluttering, I sat up, and listened to the sea. The wind

blew softly, carrying the scent of salt. Waves lapped the hull. The rigging creaked and the deck swayed. These were signs that I knew and I did not think I imagined them. But the faces!

I looked from one visage to another. Most were bearded, with savage, upthrust mustaches. Their features were harsh but showed only frank curiosity, and concern. One of the beings, whom I thought must be the captain, spoke to me. The voice was rough like the face, but the words seemed to question sympathetically. I did not, however, understand him. He tried again, more slowly.

I shook my head. "I'm sorry," I said.

He frowned, then for the first time seemed to realize that the ship still floated dead in the water. He looked about. The entire crew had crowded around us. He said nothing, but the fingers tapping slowly on his broad belt said much, and suddenly men hurried off with sheepish looks on their faces. Moments later, the sails were raised and we were once more underway. I had no idea to where.

The tallest fellow of the lot, with blond hair instead of reddish brown like the others, helped me to my feet and over to a barrel where I could sit more comfortably. A second crewman, no more than four feet tall, who I took to be the cabin boy, went below and returned moments later with a jug of yellow liquid. He smiled as he handed it to me. The small, fox-like creature lay curled up around the youth's thin shoulders, the pipes tucked into a marsupial-like pouch at its waist.

I tried to return the boy's smile and must have achieved a fairly close approximation because his own smile widened and he motioned for me to drink. I took a small swig, then a larger one. The taste was sweet as pear nectar with an undercurrent of some tangier fruit. Almost immediately I began to feel better.

The captain continued his attempts to communicate with me, using what sounded like several different languages, but I could not understand a word. Nor did he respond to the Japanese and Spanish that I tried on him. At last we both gave up and he joined me in a drink of the yellow liquid, or yellow wine I realized as the warmth began to loosen knotted muscles. The fellow gazed curiously at me as he drank; I gazed out to sea.

I thought of Bryce and wondered where he was. I did not think he was dead. He had been with me after the gate exploded, and only as we fell had I lost him. No, I did not think him dead, but he could be in danger. And I was powerless to offer aid.

In frustration, I struck a fist against my leg, spilling some wine. I realized that I was slightly drunk from the combined effects of alcohol and shock and tried to get a grip on myself. The captain looked on with sympathy and curiosity. I don't know what he thought of finding me alone in the midst of the sea. I never learned. At the time I was not thinking of it.

"Bryce," I said softly to myself. "Where the hell are you?"

Surely my brother could not have drowned. He swam like a porpoise. But then I remembered the gun that had exploded in his grip. Could he swim with such an injury? Probably. For a while. But I did not think he'd even *been* in the water. I would have seen him. Or his blood. To me, it meant that my brother lived and that he must still be on the island. But where was the island? Did this ship carry me toward it or away from it?

"Hang on, Bryce," I muttered. "I'll find you. I *swear* I'll find you."

Then the jug passed back to me and I drank again.

Other crewmen joined us occasionally. The wine went around until it was gone and a fresh jug was uncorked. And then it grew dark; the wind kicked up. I felt my eyes getting heavy and did not protest when men took my arms and helped me below decks. They took me to a cabin and a bed that was too short for me. The last did not matter for I could as easily have slept on deck. Music drifted in from somewhere, and the lad who had brought me wine blew out the lamps and began to sing, surprisingly soft. I fell asleep to his voice.

* * * * * *

I awoke to the same voice. The cabin boy stood over me, smiling, holding my clothes, which had been cleaned and freshly dried. I rose, feeling well despite the experiences of yesterday, and wondered if the wine had been laced with some revitalizing draught. Dressing quickly, I followed the boy up the stairs to the deck, picking up the scents and hearing the sounds of the sea welling up to greet me.

I stepped out into the salt air and looked into the deep, deep blue sea. It was the color of the sky over the northern Pacific near twilight when all the lighter shades have bled away. I had never seen it so dark in daytime.

It must have been midmorning judging by the brilliance of the light cast back into the air from the sea. There seemed something strange in that light, though, a tinge of unnatural color. I looked up, and the bottom fell out of the box where I'd kept my understanding of reality. The sun hung in the east where it *should* hang, but it was green, and the sky around it gleamed a bright turquoise. The shock of it staggered me as if I had been kicked in the teeth by a mule.

On the evening when I was cast into the sea by the destruction at the island temple the skies had been overcast and my mind disorientated with shock. Many things had seemed strange to me: the sea, so blue even with the sun hidden; the ship, like none seen on Earth for hundreds of years; the crew, even odder than the ship; the complete disappearance of the island when no one could have lived through an explosion great enough to hurl him so far away; and, of course, the weird being that had stood in that portal of light within the temple, the being whose death had drawn Bryce and I through that gate. All these had hinted to me of a world that was no longer as I knew it, but my heart had refused to accept the truth.

Now, in the clear green light of *this* day, I could no longer deny what I saw, what I knew. I was no longer on Earth. This may seem a needless statement to you, but to me, standing there on such a ship, with such beings around me and the light from an emerald sun falling on my upturned face, it did not seem inane. It ran over and over in my head like the continual tolling of bells.

And what of Bryce? Had he also been hurled to this

world? I hoped not but feared that he had. I had sworn to find him, but how could I accomplish that on a planet of which I knew nothing? How could I even begin to search?

Overwhelmed, I sat abruptly down on the deck. The crew gathered quickly around me, concern on their ruddy faces. Again they tried to communicate with me, but I could not understand. I just shook my head, pointed to the green sun and shook my head again.

They must have thought me mad, and I was almost ready to agree with them. Only madmen call up illusions and believe them true. Yet, I knew I was not insane. I trusted my senses. No matter how impossible this all seemed, I knew it was real. Yet that knowledge gave me little comfort. Like rats trying to escape a trap, my thoughts twisted and turned. They came in a torrent and I struggled desperately to make sense of them.

As do most youths, I had dreamed of adventures in far lands among knightly warriors and beautiful princesses. Never once had my dreams included the shock and terror that came with being torn away from all things familiar. Never once had I imagined the loneliness that struck so suddenly, or the dismay that rattled around in my head. Dream worlds are wonderful as long as they remain in your dreams and you don't have to stay in them. Now I found myself in a place far stranger than any of my dreams, and it seemed I had no choice but to stay. I knew of no way home.

After a while, I looked up to see how far the sun had traveled, an old habit. It seemed not to have moved at all, and I realized that the relationship between the sun's passage and the passage of time must not be the same here as on my home world. For a moment, a stroke of total despair shot through me. Was there nothing familiar here, nothing to count on?

I dropped my head in my hands, chewed at my lips. I felt like crying, like screaming, like banging my head against the deck. I did nothing but sit and brood, for how long I do not know. The wind on my body awakened me again to rational thought. That and the smell of the salt sea in my nostrils. These, at least, were familiar. I raised my head and drew a deep breath, then another.

We Maclangs are a practical family, or perhaps a stubborn one. Some say that we have fey souls, but if so we take them out only once in a while for a light dusting. *Now*, I would have to depend on the Maclang practicality, the Maclang stubbornness. Brooding would accomplish nothing. To find my brother and my way home I had to learn more of this world I discovered myself marooned on.

With an act of will, I made myself get up and go to the rail. I grasped the wood hard with my hands and felt the salt spray on my wrists. With my eyes closed I could easily believe that I was on my own ship, in the Pacific, on Earth. But when I opened my eyes the sun was still green and I forced myself to look about at this new earth.

I saw a place of exotic beauty. The contrasting colors of the mineral-stained sea and the turquoise sky startled the eyes, and the brilliant sun splashed sharp-edged shadows on the deck and painted green the few puffy clouds that lazed over the ship. Near the horizon, the strange sky was shot through with streaks of darker green that alternated with a flickering golden haze. Behind that haze, faintly, there came occasional flashes of intense violet light.[1]

Closer to the ship, the wind broke the sea into wavelets capped with white, and the water was very cool where it blew back across me from the prow. The air above held no birds but the ocean below teemed with fish. Everywhere, they leaped, leaving behind brief rainbows of unusual hues. I drew deep breaths, fresh and clean and rich in oxygen. Yes, this world was beautiful, and though I did not realize it my destiny lay before me.

---

[1] The name of this world in several of its tongues is Talera. That it has been artificially constructed is readily apparent when one views the night sky. The golden haze is rarely seen during the day but fills the whole horizon at night and seems to be an atmospheric shield that protects the planet's surface from poisonous clouds lying above it. One can often see monstrous displays of purple lighting that strike through those clouds to be absorbed by the shield. The sun moves beneath the shield but presents the illusion of being similar in size and distance to our own sun as viewed from Earth. It seems to rise and set normally, producing both night and day. I do not know how this has been accomplished.—Ruenn Maclang.

Perhaps half an hour I spent at the rail before striding up onto the forecastle where the captain stood scanning the sea with a scope. He lowered it and smiled broadly as I strode up. Grasping my shoulder in a comradely way, he offered me the glass and I took it and gazed out over the blue ocean. A large fish leaped, scales flashing iridescent in the sun. No land was in sight. I handed the glass back, returning the fellow's smile.

He pointed to himself and said, "Karilf," and then to me. His meaning was clear and I gave him my own name. "Renn," he repeated carefully, then grinned. His people have always called me Renn. They have some difficulty pronouncing the sound of a "u" since it is not used in their language.

Karilf pointed to the nearest sailor—the big blond fellow from the day before—and said, "Heril." Heril smiled hugely, showing white teeth that gleamed against his golden beard. He was only half a foot shorter than I but towered over the other crewmen. His chest was so broad and his limbs so muscled that he must have weighed close to my own two hundred pounds.

I wondered if Heril were of a different racial stock than the others and discovered later that he was. His were a mountain folk while lowlanders made up the rest of the ship's compliment. But Heril, I was to find, was not representative of his people, who are generally withdrawn and care little for the company of others.

Beside Heril leaned the lad who had sung for me the night before. He claimed a name that sounded like Teware. At his feet played the small, fox-like being, who was called Behlit. I knelt on one knee and held out my palm to the creature. It pulled away from me at first, hiding behind Teware's leg, but when I made no sudden moves it reached out its small hand and touched mine tentatively.

Teware encouraged it with soft cluckings, like a hen to her chicks, and after a moment it whistled something to him and ambled over gracefully to crawl up in my lap. I scratched behind its ears and it began to purr like a cat.

I stood up slowly and Behlit nestled deeper in my arms, gazing inquisitively out at the world. Thus came my introduction to a planet called Talera, and to a proud people who name themselves the Koro, and to a little creature of a species known as Toibel.

CHAPTER THREE

THE KLAR

For eleven days the wind held steady and the yellow sails carried us swiftly west. During that time something even more strange happened to the sky. The sun changed colors.[2] One morning there was a golden halo crowning the sun and a fuzzy lemon haze edging the hard emerald shadows. Over the next few days the sun became dark gold and the entire sky grew as pale as butter. The crew celebrated with music and singing, and not a few kegs of ale were broached and emptied. I helped a bit with that last.

When I asked the captain about the change in the sun he seemed stunned by my ignorance. I understood only a little of what he said but his eyes clearly questioned my sanity. Why didn't I know that the sun changes colors? That's what he wanted to ask. As of yet, I had no words to answer him. I

---

[2]Talera's sun is green in spring, gold in summer, red in fall, and bluish-white in winter. I believe the color change somehow alters the amount of heat falling on the surface and thus triggers the seasonal fluctuations.

Because Talera is an artificial world, the length of its days and years is extremely regular. Talera's day is twenty-six hours long. A year consists of 400 days. Each season is divided into three months of thirty days with ten days left over during which the sun changes color. These are times of festival and are called the spring passage, the summer passage, and so on.

A Taleran week consists of 10 days. A day is divided into twenty segments called dhaur, which are 78 minutes long. A dhaur is made up of twenty dhorrin, each about 4 minutes long. Finally, a dhorrin is divided into 100 shri, which are about two and a half seconds long.—Ruenn Maclang.

just shrugged my shoulders and wandered away.

Though I continued to worry about Bryce, the days following my arrival on Talera were pleasant enough. I even learned quite a bit of the Koro tongue during those first weeks at sea. That my survival might depend on it helped, as did being cast among a people as vocal as these.

The Koro are new to civilization and have little written language, but any common seaman is full of stories and songs enough to make one's head spin. They have a rich oral tradition and prodigious memories that would shame the scholars of many civilized nations. I could not help but absorb words and flavors and melodies, and by the end of the second week I could converse with them in simple sentences, mostly dealing with the sea or the work of sailing. From that point my vocabulary expanded rapidly.

It was not so easy to adjust to Talera in other ways. The foods. The wines. The clothing. All were different than I was used to. And the night was strangest of all. There were no stars overhead, and I missed them, but the night sky of Talera was certainly beautiful. Making up for the lack of stars were four moons, and whenever those orbs were not aloft the golden haze of the atmospheric shield played lightly in the heavens.

At times the vast cloud cover kept at bay by that screen lay quiescent, but at other times the whole horizon would be lit by monstrous displays of purple and pale lighting. The skies of Talera were seldom dark, except when local storms brewed beneath the shield and the air filled with rain.

On the sixteenth day after the Koro rescued me we finally sighted land, a haze-shrouded island that jutted like a worn tooth out of the ocean. The crew let out a cheer and, as if in response, the ship leaped ahead. We sailed in close to the shore where dark trees overhung the sea, trailing limbs and vines in the water. Life teemed, none of it silent. Birds and other...things flitted among the leaves, filling the air with raucous voices. Frogs and toads, or something akin to them, hung like multicolored grapes from the trees and swarmed in their myriads along freshets that ran from the interior. Along with those streams came a breeze that tingled my nostrils with jasmine, lavender, eucalyptus, and a hundred other odors for which I had no names.

Insects buzzed everywhere, into eyes and ears and even mouths left open too long. They made a film across the surface of the water that formed a rich stew for the flashing silver fish that hunted the murky shallows. I itched to have a pole in my hand and to try my luck at some of the denizens of the Taleran waters, but we did not stop for fishing.

We turned south and hugged the coast in the intense heat of early afternoon, and in a dhaur we passed the jungle by and rounded a headland into a blue-steel lagoon. Three ships were there, all of black wood, with violet sails and two rows of ebon oars shipped in the ports. The ships stood with demon figureheads catching the sun at their prows, and black flags hung at the masts. Smoke rose from the shore beyond the ships, dark against the pale gold of the sky.

Silence fell across the Koro. I stood beside the captain on the forward deck and heard him mutter a word under his breath, a curse, I thought, or perhaps the name of a god. The word was "Klar." In a moment that whisper echoed from men all about me and I knew that whatever a Klar was, it was a thing of terror.

Activity exploded on the black ships. Anchor chains rattled as they were drawn in and oars were suddenly thrust outboard. Our own ship lost headway as panic coursed freely through the crew. Then Karilf leaped down among his men. Cursing and shoving, he yanked them out of their fear and sent them scurrying to their stations. The ship wallowed and then recovered herself. Sails that had been partially furled as we approached an expected anchorage were loosed. We leaped ahead, turning across the wind and away from the island.

We ran as if hell followed after us, but those who crewed the dark craft had scented us and came on swiftly. I marveled at the discipline that allowed those sailors to get their longships into motion so easily. And their ships were faster than our own.

We started the race with half a mile head start but our pursuers closed the gap rapidly and the captain soon realized that we couldn't outrun them. He snapped an order and a dozen crewmen rushed below to return with swords and shields, lances and axes, which were distributed among the Koro. There were longbows as well, with scarlet arrows fletched with the yellow feathers of some Taleran bird, and crossbows of blond wood with silver-headed quarrels.

I took a crossbow and a sword. The blade was not as heavy as I was accustomed to but I hoped the techniques of its use would not be too dissimilar. As for the crossbow, well, I had used them for hunting and knew their power. I slipped a bright quarrel into the mechanism and locked it down.

Whoever was closing on us must have been an enemy that the Koro much feared. I had seen the panic in their eyes and Karilf obviously did not intend to be taken without a fight. I did not think the Koro were easily frightened. Strictly speaking, of course, this was not my battle. For all I knew, the beings who chased us had good reasons for doing so. But I did not believe it. Nor would it have mattered. The Koro had saved my life. They had fed me and befriended me and I had grown to enjoy their company. I would fight with them when it came to that. I have many faults but ingratitude is not one of them.

The Koro were skilled sailors, and we held the enemy vessels back for a time despite their speed. We danced and dodged across the waves as a fox would dance before hounds. But our pursuers were not hounds. Their ships hunted us like wolves, acting in concert to cut off every avenue of escape and pull us down.

They closed, and soon I caught my first glimpse of a Klar. At the prow of our leading pursuer leaned a being in black and russet leathers, with a blood-red shield on its left arm and an ochre belt, from which hung the pommel of a black sword, encircling its waist. It was neither Human nor Koro, but a reptile, though one very different from the beast Bryce and I had encountered in that temple on Earth; it seemed ages ago.

The Klar stood well over six feet in height and probably weighed close to three hundred pounds. Its skin gleamed with slick gray scales and muscles bulged in ropes beneath the oily hide. Its features were human-like, though exaggerated in size. Its bullet shaped head was hairless. A tail flicked up behind it, thin and pale like that of a rat. Beneath a snarling image of a two-faced demon the Klar lounged at perfect ease, and above that figurehead whipped a black flag with an oddly shaped skull in its center. The flag was so similar to that which once graced pirate ships on Earth—the one called the Jolly Roger—that I was startled.

The Klar seemed to sense my gaze. It raised its red shield in acknowledgment and we were close enough for me to see its teeth flash in an almost human smile. I tightened my grip on the sword and crossbow. We would fight. Aye, we would fight. And soon the chase ended and the fight was upon us.

A longship pulled to either side of us. A wooden corvus, bound with iron, fell from each to smash through the railing of our ship and embed their metal spikes in her deck. Her torn planking screeched as if in agony.

From the outset our forces were divided as boarding parties rushed across each wooden bridge. Arrows and bolts flashed from our ranks and struck. A few went true and Klar staggered and flipped over the railing into the sea, but most rebounded from high held shields. Our enemy did not return fire and at first I wondered why.

Then they tore in among us and I had no time to wonder. Steel flashed and turned red in the yellow-edged shadows of the Taleran sun. I triggered the crossbow and the brass-headed quarrel took a swiftly moving Klar through the chest. It rocked on its feet and fell on its face. Its gray-green flesh rippled and began to change colors, running from gray, to orange, to red, and then to pale chalk. But there was little time to watch the dead.

I fired the crossbow a second time but the bolt shrieked wildly off an iron shield and splashed in the sea. An axe sliced through the air toward my head. I slipped beneath the blow and punched upward with the crossbow. It caught the Klar beneath the chin, opening a gash through which crimson spurted. The beast staggered back, tail lashing. I reversed the bow and struck again, shattering the wooden stock on the Klar's thick skull. It went down.

The broken bow went to my left hand as the sword was ripped free by my right. I caught a Klar blade on the crossbow stock, then smashed a boot into the side of the pirate's knee. Bone snapped and the beast fell. For the first time I heard a Klar voice. Its scream ached high and shrill, like burning trees. Even in falling it slashed out and I leaped madly aside to avoid its blade.

It seemed for a moment as if we would hold, until Klar reinforcements boiled over each corvus and leaped in among us. Our defense shattered under that onslaught. The Koro fought valiantly but were no match for the supple strength and blinding speed of the raiders. They died bravely.

Out of the corner of an eye, I saw Karilf struck down by a double bitted axe that opened his skull to the shoulders. Beside him, Heril roared madly with anger and drove his own steel axe into the Klar killer. Suddenly, lead weighted nets flashed overhead and Heril went down, struggling. Other nets filled the air and then the Klar began using the butts of swords and axes to knock men unconscious.

Now I realized why the raiders hadn't used arrows on us. The Klar wanted captives. Were they slavers as well as pirates? I had seen slaves in the orient. I did not wish to become one.

A net whirled over me and I ducked under it. My sword took a second net out of the air. A Klar loomed to my right, naked torso glistening with sweat, naked steel slicing down. I turned the stroke on my sword and drove my own steel into its chest. It staggered back, spilling blood over its hand as it grabbed at the wound.

Instantly, a second Klar stood before me. Its sword glittered as red as the shield on its arm. Again it saluted me with that shield, as it had done when standing at the prow of its own ship.

"You fight well for someone who will soon be chattel," it said in the Koro tongue.

We locked eyes for a moment. "I suppose we'll see," I said.

The being chuckled, flicked its tail at me...and leaped. Its movements were those of a striking cobra, swift and hard. The sword shimmered in its left hand. I parried one blow and jumped aside. Our blades crossed again, and then again. The beast was better than I with a sword, I realized, but it did not

37

wish to kill me. It drove me back until the black strands of a net, stinking with fish, curled about me. Other strands took my legs and I crashed heavily to the deck on my left side. Bells rang in my head.

The sounds of battle died away. I did not struggle in the net, for that would only draw the strands tighter and I have no love for confinement. A Klar warrior kicked the sword from my hand. He said something to the others and a raw, aching laughter boomed.

Other slavers went about with daggers and began to dispatch those too badly injured to be saleable. I forgot my dislike for confinement then and struggled, but to no avail. I could not even avoid the freshly spilled blood as it ran down the deck to pool beneath my shoulder. In my nostrils, the stench of it was like copper and fate.

CHAPTER FOUR

SLAVES OF TALERA

The pirates took the captured Koro ship back to the blue cove and beached it there on the white sand. Blood clotted that sand. Not from our crew. We were left wrapped in our nets but were hauled off the boat and dumped unceremoniously down.

Smoke still rose on the island but now it stained a sky full of approaching evening. I saw that it rose from the embers of a torched village, a Koro village, judging by other slaves who milled about miserably within a tall enclosure of pointed stakes. Sharp wires stretched between the stakes and guards strolled about. Almost all the prisoners were women and children. I wondered if any of them belonged to the men of our ship.

The Klar are a violent race, savage and cruel, but they are quite efficient at mastering their chattel. A beast with silver scales strode by the line of new captives, occasionally reaching down and marking one or another with black greasepaint. I was thus marked. I turned my head and found Teware beside me. He, too, was marked with black. He seemed frightened but I was glad to see him alive.

"Behlit?" I asked him, not seeing his Toibel friend.

He only shook his head and could not return the smile that I tried to force for his benefit. Little else could I do to comfort him.

Soon, we were removed from the nets and added to coffles, our arms bound behind us. Our feet were left free but we were linked together at the necks with just enough slack to provide us with some movement. All those marked with black were chained together. Being tallest, I ended up at the head of the chain with Heril placed behind me. Poor Teware would be far down toward the end of the line. Most of us just stared at the dirt. Already, many had taken on the demeanor of longtime slaves, with shuffling feet and dulled eyes.

For what seemed like hours, we were forced to stand with the weight of irons on our bodies and our arms tied. But it could not have been so long for there was still daylight left when I at last shook off my lethargy and looked around. The sound of splashing oars caught my attention.

A ship's boat drew in to shore. It was manned by Klar but there were others aboard who were not of that race. One was a Human male, the first Human I had seen on Talera. The other was a young woman who looked to be about nineteen or twenty. She was beautiful.

If I say that Talera went away from me then and that I could not remember the pain of my bruises and cuts, I am not far from wrong. If I say that I momentarily forgot the bonds I wore, I speak only the truth. I wonder if for every man there is a woman who is to him pure enchantment. Surely, the perfection of this girl's face and form were no more perfect objectively than that of many another woman on Earth and Talera. But to me there could be no comparison. At the risk of repeating myself, I say again that she was beautiful.

Around her slender form a white gown floated like a rapture, molded to her by the wind. Her hair glowed raven black against the silk, and fell to her shoulders in misted waves that danced about her face. It danced about features of ivory beauty, about high cheekbones and slightly hollowed cheeks, about a slim nose and lips that shone dark against her too-pale skin.

The girl's arms were bare, as were her feet. At her wrists and ankles, and about her throat, gleamed the silver of chains. So, she too was a slave. I am not sure why my heart pounded in anger at that, but a flush rose in my face and my fists clenched behind me.

Not wishing to be caught staring at her, I looked away. But again and again my eyes were drawn back. Once our glances crossed and a shiver ran up my spine and tingled my scalp. Her irises smoldered as dark blue as the Taleran Sea. It was I who broke the gaze.

Only then did I look at her companion. He was tall, and handsome in a strutting, arrogant way. His skin was darker than the girl's but still light, as if he had spent little time under the sun. He wore a sword, a rapier with an ornate hilt, sheathed in a gilded scabbard, and he was dressed in leather breeches and an overshirt of some silken material that had been dyed green. Gems and silver hung from his ears, and flashed on his chest and from around his neck. He wore gray leather gloves, the color of his eyes. He was not a slave. The Klar sailors stepped from his path briskly and leaped to when he gave an order.

This dandy stopped in front of us, the girl only a step or two behind. He said something loudly—I think for the benefit of the girl—and his laughter was ugly. At the time I did not understand his words, but Heril, locked in chains behind me, understood, and he explained them to me much later. I will translate them for you because they have a bearing on this story.

"So, these are the scum we bested," was what he said.

I did not remember seeing him on the deck when the corvus was dropped and the Klar charged in among the Koro with their axes. The sword at his waist did not look as if it had been recently cleansed of blood. But, to tell the truth, I did not pay much attention to him then. My eyes kept looking beyond his shoulder at the girl. She looked back at me and he saw our glances.

I do not know what filled my gaze but there was only kindness and sympathy in hers. But he saw our glances exchange and thought something different. He turned and backhanded her across the face. Her head jerked to the side and blood trickled from one corner of her lips, but she did not whimper, and I saw those blue eyes go very cold.

He turned back to me and raised his hand; I kicked him in the belly. He let out a woof and fell forward onto his knees. His eyes bulged and he lost his dinner all over the sand. I would have kicked him again but the guards leaped upon me with their staves, sending a rain of blows falling across my shoulders and arms. I heard the girl shout something and Heril later said that she yelled at them to stop, but of course they did not. Why should they listen to a slave?

The man staggered up and came at me, his hand rising with something dark, a quirt or a cane, in it. Desperately, I jerked my head to the side as the blow slashed down, but my movements were constrained by my neck chain and the object caught me on the left cheek, laying the skin open to the bone. The cut burned like a sudden fire; blood ran warm on my face. I hooked a boot behind the fellow's leg and heaved, and he went down on his rump with a loud screech. He started to rise again and the guards got hold of me solidly and slammed me to my knees. They held me immobile.

The dandy's face purpled with anger and he drew his fancy sword. It went aloft and a twinkling ray of light from the golden sun burst along it. Up and up it went, but before it could fall a slim form in white leaped and grabbed that arm and dragged the sword down.

The man hurled the girl away and would have killed me then, but another hand took his wrist, this one covered with scales. It was the Klar I had last fought with aboard the Koro ship, he who carried the blood-shield. He was not, I thought, the chief commander of the Klar. But he *was* a beast with power. The purple died in the man's face and he quickly recovered himself.

"What do you here, Lord Durhain?" the Klar asked. "I will have no killing of my slaves."

"This animal attacked me!" Durhain said, pointing at me.

The Klar facial features are not unlike those of Humans, and though they are not given often to laughter I saw the smirk on the Klar captain's face. A half naked, unarmed slave, chained in a coffle and with his hands bound behind him, had leaped on a warrior armed with a sword! Of course! Yet it was, I suppose, near the truth.

"I demand retribution," Durhain said.

The Klar looked from Durhain to me. I saw the calculation in his eyes as he weighed the worth of a new slave against the worth of a Human who obviously had some influence among them.

"Very well, my Lord," he said soothingly. "But paid in

42

blood, not life. Fifteen lashes from the snake." That was not the term he used but was the type of whip he meant.

"Agreed," Durhain said, though he did not seem pleased.

The Klar gestured to his guards and I was jerked roughly to my feet. My neck chains were removed, my hands unbound. A nearby tree made a convenient whipping post. Two pirates tied me facing the trunk, my hands above my head, the bark pressing so close into my cheek that I could smell dust and pollen. I do not know what I expected. Pain, yes. But not the agony that followed. It was like all the pain of the world coalesced into a few moments of time, into fifteen strokes of the whip.

The first blow laid a razor-trail across my shoulders and down my back, and smashed me forward into the tree against which I was bound. Rough bark cut into my face and chest. I tasted blood where I had bitten my lip to keep from screaming. I had told myself I would not scream and I did not, but it was among the most difficult things I have ever done. The second blow hurt far worse than the first, and the third fell quickly, and the fourth. There was room for one thought, not to cry out, and then even that disappeared and there was only red-hot agony. But fifteen lashes do not take much physical time. They were soon finished, though for many years after I wondered if they would ever be over.

I stood until they cut me loose, then slid down the tree to the earth. Blood dripped on the bark. Lord Durhain went away smirking, dragging the girl after him. She looked back once but it was growing dark and I could not make out her expression.

The Klar with the blood-shield squatted beside me. "You should thank me, Human," it said. "I saved your life."

I did not speak.

"Your named is Ruenn is it not?"

Still I did not speak.

The beast smiled. "You may be a fool, Human, but I must admit that you're sturdy. And you fight well. It may be that I have need of such skills."

It gestured to the guards standing about. "Take this one to the ship and put him in the extra cabin. Send the woman to tend him. She is of his own kind and should know what to do. Lord Durhain need not be informed. Tell him I want him ashore. I'll think of a reason when he gets here."

The guards saluted, fists across chests, and dragged me off.

CHAPTER FIVE

PRELUDE TO A STORM

"Lay back warrior or you'll open your wounds again."

I allowed a slender hand to push me down on the bunk. I rested on my side, my back raw from the whip, my stomach torn by the jagged bark of the tree to which I had been bound. The left side of my face was numb from the blow of Durhain's quirt.

A Klar longship moved gently beneath me where we lay at anchor in the still cove at the island. It was night. Lanterns had been lit against the darkness. The woman's hands were soft and deft on my injuries but still her touch brought pain.

"I'm sorry," she said, seeing me wince. She spoke in the Koro tongue, which is commonly used among seafaring peoples of Talera.

"No need," I said. "Having them treated is nothing compared to having them."

She smiled at that.

"I owe you my thanks, lady," I said.

"For what?" she asked.

"For my life. If you had not grabbed Durhain's arm...." I did not finish.

"I am glad that you live," she said, "but you owe me nothing. Your life would not have been in danger were it not for me."

I made no comment to that but thought that she was wrong. Lord Durhain needed no reasons for his cruelty, and if he had then I'd provided him with one by kicking him in

45

the gut.

I smiled at that.

"May I ask your name?" I said.

"It is Rannon," she said. "And yours?"

"Ruenn Maclang."

"An odd name. But I like it."

"And yours is very beautiful," I told her.

"Thank you," she said, amusement tingeing her voice.

"There," she said, stepping back. "All cleaned and bandaged. You had best lie still for a while, though, so you won't start bleeding again."

"I feel much better," I told her. "Thank you."

She laughed.

"What is so funny?" I asked her, surprised.

"Us," she said. "Two prisoners on a Klar pirate ship. Our future in doubt. Yet we speak as if we had just met at a ball and were strolling through sweet scented gardens with not a care in the world."

The humor of the situation struck me and I laughed with her. It hurt so much that I quickly stopped, and she apologized for causing me pain. I didn't mind; to hear her laugh was worth it.

When we had been silent for a moment, I heard her sigh and she moved toward the door.

"I must return now," she said. "Durhain will be back soon and will be furious if he finds out I've been gone."

"You are his slave then?" The words blurted out of my mouth, and at once I wished they had not been said.

She stopped smiling and I saw the cold look come again into her eyes. "His captive, perhaps. But I will never be his slave. I will die first."

"Do not die, Rannon," I said. "His day will come."

"Yes, I know," she said. "I'll see to it."

I thought then that I would not wish her for an enemy.

"Goodbye, Ruenn Maclang," she said. "Perhaps we will meet again."

"I believe we will," I said.

She smiled and slipped out in a rustle of white silk. Her scent lingered, clean and lavender-cool, leaving me to feel very much alone.

46

A short time later a Klar came into the cabin bringing food and a little wine. I ate and drank sparingly. The wine must have been drugged, however, for I soon passed into a sound sleep.

A change in the motion of the ship awakened me. I knew that rise and fall. We were at sea. I started to get up and gasped with pain. My movements would have to be slow for a while, I decided. Pulling on my trousers carefully, I shuffled to the door. A guard stood there with an axe. He would not let me pass, but only moments later there entered the Klar who had stopped Durhain from killing me. He carried a covered plate that steamed and tantalized. My mouth watered, angering me.

"I see you're able to move about," the Klar captain said, setting the food on a small table. "You recover rapidly. Good."

"We've set sail," I accused him.

"Yes," he agreed. "Our holds are full."

"With slaves, no doubt," I snapped.

His upper lip quirked. "Of course."

"Where are you taking us?"

He answered, as if it amused him to indulge a slave. "The ones aboard *this* ship are being taken to auction. We have need of gold."

"Those marked with black," I guessed, remembering the Klar who had daubed Heril, Teware, and myself with dark grease.

"Yes. And the others will be taken to the homeland to serve us there."

"What of Durhain then? And his captive? Do they go with us?"

"Why do you ask?"

"Would you not be anxious to know the whereabouts of a man who wished you dead?"

He smiled. "I might. Somehow, I don't think you are. You'll have to learn to hide your thoughts better, Human. They are quite transparent. Durhain and the female slave, or *captive* if you prefer, are going to the homeland. Perhaps if you are agreeable you might get to see them again. Or at least one of them again."

"Agreeable about what?"

"What I've come to speak to you about."

I waited for him to go on, saying nothing.

"My name is Jask," he added after a moment. "Only Jask. You have seen my shield and know that it carries no heraldry?"

The last was a question. I did remember his shield, blood-red and empty of device, and now that he spoke of it I seemed to recall that the shields of many of the other slavers had borne embossments on their surfaces.

"So?" I asked.

He smiled mirthlessly. "It means that I am without lineage, without a clan to call my own. When my ancestors settled our present homeland there were two hundred families, their retainers, and slaves. Families died out, alliances formed, allegiances changed. There are now one hundred and twenty clans in whose hands all power is consolidated.

"There are, as well, many thousands of others who have no direct or legal claim to membership in one of the clans. These are mostly descendants of the old retainers, criminals who have lost their rank, or the illegitimate daughters and sons of clan nobles. I am from the last group. We are called Keshaki. We have few rights and little protection under clan law, save what we earn with our swords.

"There are many who are angered by this. I have been a leader among them and have made enemies for it. I do not think the clan chieftains will imprison me. I am popular among the Keshaki. But it was sudden that I was chosen for this journey and there are warriors among my crew whom I do not know."

"You fear assassination," I said.

He nodded. "I need men around me I can trust, who owe their allegiance only to me."

"So you find them among slaves?"

"I find them wherever I can."

"Why come to me?"

"I fought you and you are skilled with weapons. Too, you have courage, even though it nearly got you killed."

"There is more," I said, seeing it in him.

"Yes," he said. "I think you are alone."

48

He was right. Even though I had made friends among the Koro I was still more alone on this strange world than Jask or anyone else here could imagine. Except, perhaps, for my brother Bryce.

"I will not expect you to fight with me for nothing," Jask continued. "There will be wine. And women if you wish. In time even your freedom. I treat those who are loyal to me quite well."

"And if I refuse?"

"I could have you beaten," he said, "but I won't. I find that men, whether Klar or Human, perform better when rewarded than when coerced. However, I will tell you that life fighting for me is infinitely preferable to many other forms of slavery."

It was in my heart to refuse, but then I thought of what he had said, especially of freedom. There were other slaves aboard this ship, Heril and Teware among them. I, too, was a slave but was not chained with the rest as cargo. Perhaps I could make use of my greater freedom.

"How do you know I won't run you through the first time I'm given a sword?" I asked Jask.

He laughed. "You will be guarded at first. I trust you do not wish to die. Besides, I'm still your master with a blade."

Yes, he was that.

"All right," I said. "I'll fight for you."

"Excellent! We'll begin your training in a few days. For now you must rest."

He turned to go and I stopped him. "May I go on deck, *master*?" I asked.

"Of course," he said. "Under guard. And you needn't call me *master*. Lord Jask will do."

He smiled as he spoke and I think maybe my sarcasm was not lost on him. This was odd for a Klar, I learned. They do not often think like Humans. But then, Lord Jask did not seem typical of his race. In fact, under other circumstances I could have liked him. He went out, strutting arrogantly.

I thought, then, of the slaves below me in the hold. No doubt it was dark there, and damp. My fists clenched; my fingers itched for a weapon. Given a chance, I would have the slaves free and we would take this ship. And then? Well, then we would take whatever other ships we needed as we freed our friends, even if it meant venturing into the heart of the Klar homeland. Perhaps you see that I was still quite naive to the ways of Talera. At the time it did not seem that it would be so difficult.

One thought disturbed me, though. Lord Jask. He was Klar. I had seen his blade gleaming red with Koro blood, and at his order I'd been beaten. Yet, I admitted that he had probably saved my life and I did not think I would like to kill him. That is, if I could.

There was also the matter of my word. I believed that he had been honest in what he had told me about himself and his people. I had not been so honest in saying that I would fight for him. My *only* reason for doing so had been to maintain what freedom of action I had until such time as I had loosed my friends. But....

Finally, I shrugged the thoughts away. I would decide what to do when the time came. For now, I needed to heal as quickly as possible. I sat down and began to eat the breakfast stew that Jask had supplied me with. It was rich and aromatic, and full of chunks of meat whose origins I decided not to question.

CHAPTER SIX

STORMS OF A DIFFERENT COLOR

We drifted alone on the sea beneath a heavy sun. To the south and west, peaks of cloud towered into the air, white above and gray beneath, and the sky overhead was tinged with green despite the sun of gold. Talera was not my world and this was not my sea, but I knew the signs. To the south of us a storm gathered its might.

The Klar longship on which I stood moved under power, but not the power of the wind. That had not blown for three days. We traveled by the strength of oars. I could hear the thrust of them against the waves and feel the rhythm of the ship's movement, so different than movement under sail. Too, there was the count of cadence, and, occasionally, the snap of the whip as a slave slacked at his oar.

These slaves were not the newly acquired Koro. Those were being saved for the auction block. The oar-slaves had been brought from the Klar homeland specifically for this purpose. Their lot was harsh. I wondered how many were dying in the heat.

Lord Jask did not seem particularly solicitous of the rowers' well-being. After all, they were but chattel. "Watch yourself, Ruenn," he called, and leaped toward me with his sword flashing.

I parried and riposted. He avoided easily and ducked under my strike. My own blade dropped and the two swords met and locked. We withdrew. There came no clang of metal on metal for both the tips and edges of our weapons were covered in cork.

51

Jask stepped back. "Better," he said, "but your guard is weak. You have much to learn."

I did not dispute him, for it was true.

We stood on deck, clad only in linen loincloths, our bodies bathed in sweat and with swords in our hands. For a Taleran week (ten days) we'd sailed west with a fair wind, the swift longship covering many verlangs (one verlang = about one and one-half miles). And for three days we had been becalmed and moved only by the power of oars.

As I said, our ship was alone. The other two warships and the Koro prize had turned south the fourth day out while we continued to the west. Aboard those vessels had been many Koro, some who had become my friends and others whom I did not know. And on one of them rode a girl who constantly pierced my thoughts. They all went south to slave for the Klar while the Koro aboard this ship were being taken to the coast of Thresh to be sold for red gold. I would not see the auction block. As a fighting slave, a *rahnvin*, I was too useful to sell. This, I had learned from Jask.

Angrily, I raised my sword and launched an attack against the pirate captain. I surprised him and for a moment drove him back with a blur of steel. Our blades touched and danced. We strained against each other, and then I was hurled back by his superior strength.

"Excellent, Ruenn," he said. "Excellent! You begin to enter into the spirit of things. Now, on guard."

I prepared to meet him.

Thirteen Taleran days had passed since my beating. My wounds were nearly healed. I was not yet at full strength but was well enough to take up my duties as Lord Jask's sword-slave, or at least my training. I was not yet trusted alone. Nor did I carry a weapon except during our practice bouts on the quarterdeck.

Occasionally, the Koro were brought up from below and allowed to exercise their cramped muscles. The Klar wanted them healthy for their sale. From the porthole of Jask's cabin, I often watched Heril, Teware, and others that I knew. But none of them saw me. This, Lord Jask would not permit, and I did not gainsay him. I did not wish them to see me because I could not bear the thought of them believing me to be a traitor, even if the evidence seemed to indicate that they were right.

There was much difference, of course, between the Koro and the galley slaves who rowed the ship. The Koro were fresh to slavery while many of the latter had probably been in fetters for years. They would not be sold in Thresh. Their place was at the oars, forever. They would row until they died.

Whenever the Koro were brought on deck I saw them looking into the open rowing-hold at the other slaves. Some looked with pity and others with disgust. They stared at the filth and the broken bodies, the filmed eyes and toothless mouths. And after a while I saw the pity and disgust turn to fear as they realized how easy it would be to end up the same. Grown men wept then, while boys stood dry-eyed and defiant.

I had known of slavery and of its horrors from Earth, but I learned something else in seeing the oarsmen aboard Jask's ship. I learned finally the utter strangeness of this world that I found myself on, a lesson I'd not soon forget.

Full Humans were among the galley slaves, but there were also half a dozen other races, some far weirder than the Koro or Klar. There were Vhichang: tall and avian, with a light dusting of downy feathers under which rippled lean muscle. There were Kaldi: broad and stocky, covered with fur and with the faces of friendly bears. There were the members of several races called Llurns, who look Human except for exotic skin and hair colors, which are gold or green or jet black with silver, and their eyes, which are lavender and yellow and argent gleams. And, finally, there were the Nokarra, who walked on two legs and moved like giant tailless cats with fangs in their eyes.

All bore scars and the marks of manacles and whips. They made a savage and barbaric sight, but most had been captive for a long time and their eyes were dull and their spirits bent. All, that is, except for the Nokarra. I thought those beings would be hard to break. Here and there were a few others with pride left in their bodies. I did not know if they were stronger than their fellows or only new to the benches.

Again, Jask and I engaged, our swords weaving in and out like dueling adders. We were not using shields, and I had to leap and skip to avoid Jask's swift blade. I was tiring. Perhaps I was not as recovered as I had thought.

The two of us practiced alone on the quarterdeck beneath a stifling heat. The rest of Jask's guards, all Klar, had gone forward to help prepare the sails. There was still no wind, but low swells had started to rock the ship from the south and the wind would not be long in following. We would need to take instant advantage of that breeze if we were to try and outrun the storm. I did not care for the looks of the sky but Jask did not seem overly concerned.

"I've seen storms before," he said. "On guard."

Once more we engaged. For three days I had worked at swords with my Klar master, longer each session, and much of my old skill had begun to return. There had been a time on Earth when I was well known as a fencer in parts of California, and I found, to my pleasant surprise, that I was close to holding my own with Jask. He was stronger than I, and quicker because of my wounds, but there were still a few things he didn't know. There were little tricks of swordplay that I had picked up in the Orient, but I did not use them. Now was not the time.

My father had been quite a poker player before he met my mother. He once told me: "You have to show your opponent enough to make him bet, but never show him all you have until the money is on the table." I had no intention of showing Jask everything I had. Yet.

The Klar stepped back, breathing hard. He wiped sweat from his eyes. "You are good, Ruenn. Much better than I expected."

I looked at him, and then beyond him to where I'd heard a faint sound.

"We shall work well together," Jask continued, smiling.

The sound repeated, a scuffling, as of leather on wood. The faintest of breezes stirred. On it rode the musky scent of Klar. But Jask was not between me and the wind. He had moved to lean over the rail.

"Ware your back, Lord," I said, and five Klar came over the edge of the quarterdeck and hurled themselves upon us.

There were, I had learned, various races of Klar, just as there are for Humans. These five differed clearly from Jask. Where his skin was dark gray, almost black, theirs glowed a dull green. They were smaller than Jask, all of a size, their features thinner and more aquiline. They each carried a yellow shield with the symbol of a coiled snake and a sword embossed on the lacquered surface. This was not, as I at first thought, a clan crest. It was an assassin's mark.

My warning barely gave us enough time to tear the cork shells from our blades, but we met our would-be killers with naked steel brandished in our fists. Yes, there were five of them, five sent after one, but I suppose they had expected to have to deal with guards. They must have considered their god to have smiled on them when they found Jask alone, save for a Human slave.

They discounted me at first and that was a mistake. One died quickly for it when he trusted in his shield to block me while he stabbed at Jask. I drove my sword beneath his defense deep into his body. It came out red. As I may have noted, Klar bleed the same color as men.

Jask was their goal and the assassins pressed him hard. He was driven back against the rail, his sword barely keeping wicked points at bay. I came in from the side. A Klar beast turned on me, thinking to deal with me first. His blade slithered out and I went past it, my own steel blurring with speed. The tip slid his shield and pricked him good, and when his guard dropped I whipped the brand up in a backhand blow that tore away his throat. His rapier pitched from dead fingers, arced over the rail, and splashed in the sea. It left one gleam in the air, a dull one for the sun had been swallowed by clouds.

Then our foes were on the defensive. As I engaged a third attacker, Jask pushed away from the rail and charged the other two like a maddened bull. A sword nicked his shoulder and then his own heavy blade sliced through the air. An assassin went down, nearly decapitated. Jask's sword returned to parry a thrust and he followed with an overhand strike that drove ten inches of razored steel through another beast's chest. The point came out the thing's back along with a trickle of blood.

My opponent tried to run, little realizing in his panic that there was nowhere aboard the ship to hide. Jask drew a black dagger from a scabbard at his waist and hurled it. It took the fleeing Klar between the shoulders and went in to the hilt. The beast pitched forward off the quarterdeck and thudded loudly to the planks below. The corpses began to change color, their flesh running through the rainbow before fading to white. I have seen fish on Earth who show such a phenomenon.

Jask's gaze met mine. The Klar captain was spattered with his enemies' blood but he smiled. He slapped me on the back, making me wince.

"Now that was a rip was it not, Ruenn? I knew I had chosen well in picking you out."

I did not speak. My thoughts were on something else. I could have killed Jask then and blamed it on the assassins. The tip of my sword rose, seemingly on its own, but I forced it down again. That would not free the slaves or bring back those who had died, and the next captain might be worse. Then the moment was gone as guards swarmed around us, turning over the dead to view our assailants.

I ignored the bustle and looked out to sea. The swells were growing beneath the ship and a stray gust of wind tugged at my hair. The storm was coming. For three days it had brewed, three days in which our ship crossed still waters beneath green-tinged skies. I did not think we had much longer to wait for its arrival. And I was right.

Within an hour of the fight the storm reached out and smashed us with a heavy fist. Clouds conquered the sky, veined with lightning as they roiled and heaved and drew down a purple darkness. Lanterns were lit as if it were night. Ropes were strung from bow to stern. The wind howled up from the south, bringing swells that were capped thickly with white. But we held our own against them. The oars were shipped and we hauled up canvas to keep us underway. We ran before the gale.

The wind brought hail and threw it down like marbles on the deck, and it lashed across us with rain. I stood with Jask near the stern, near the rudder. Four men, four Klar, held the steering oar and held it well. It moaned and creaked but kept us true.

The storm did not care for that. Oh, I know storms have no feelings, but out in the middle of this strange ocean it became easy to forget that. It seemed to me that the wind hesitated for a moment, like a predator about to leap. Then it raged upon us with fresh frenzy. Canvas ripped away and could not be replaced. Just out of my reach, a Klar missed his grip on a rope and was hurtled overboard. There was no possibility of rescue.

The waves grew higher; the storm seemed berserk. The galley slaves were ordered to row again in a desperate attempt to keep the ship from foundering. Even the four Klar could not hold the steering oar, and Jask and I joined them at it. We threw our backs into it and stayed the course. The strain ripped at my arms and shoulders. Blisters rose and burst on my hands, slicking the wood with blood. I heard a crack and thought the masts had gone, but it was only the whip of canvas, torn free by the wind. It sailed overhead, outspread like the wings of a giant bat.

"If the masts go she'll never hold together!" I screamed in Jask's ear.

"She'll hold!" he shouted back. "She'll hold!" Then he muttered something I didn't catch. I wondered if it were prayer or a curse. I said a few prayers myself, for the ship, and for the Koro below deck who must be sick with fear. Then I threw more of myself against the oar.

I do not know how long we held there. We held until our muscles began to quiver and our spines to bend, and still we held, more by will than by strength. We held until a wave came up behind us like none I had ever seen. I sensed it, and looked up, and screamed a warning as the wall of black water trembled at the brink and then came down. The masts went all at once and the rudder snapped. I was hurled aside and just managed to clutch a rope and hang on, a rope so taut that it thrummed. A Klar went by me and I made a grab for him and missed. His mouth gaped open but I could not hear his terror.

The ship wallowed beneath the wave and keeled over onto her side. But like a bear shaking off hounds she shook off the water and rose. I applauded her and her builders. But

57

how long could it last? The oars had splintered. Slaves had been maimed—or killed at their posts by pieces of broken wood driven like spears by the wind. The port railing had caved in. With masts and rudder gone, the ship had slewed sideways in the water.

Suddenly, Jask was beside me. I did not know how he had survived. He caught my arm. "Abandon ship!" he shouted. "We'll break in half under this pounding!" Then he grabbed a line and began hauling himself forward.

"The slaves!" I screamed after him. "What of the slaves?" But he did not hear. Or did not care.

I knew only too well what the pirates intended to do: cut their losses, let the slaves drown. I should have expected as much. They were Klar, after all.

Frantically, I began to work my way forward. The ship reeled drunkenly beneath me and every few feet I had to stop and hang on as water ripped across the deck to drag me away. I crawled under a broken mast and suddenly found myself amidships. Through the haze of foam and mist filling the air, I saw boats being lowered. Jask was in the middle of a roiling mass of panic-stricken Klar. He alone seemed calm. He glimpsed me in the spray and waved a hand for me to join him, but I shook my head and motioned below. I did not wait to see his response.

In a lull between successive waves, I ran across the deck and leaped down into the rowing-hold. I landed badly, sprawling across something soft, something dead. I scrambled away from the body and looked about. Oars had snapped like matchwood throughout the open hold. Arms and legs and necks were twisted to odd angles, but here and there amid the floating wreckage, beings lived. Even above the waves and wind I could hear their moans and screams.

One man, a Green Llurn, lay almost at my feet. Debris and chains held him down, and the water had risen to his chest. His eyes looked wide at me but he made no sound. I cast about for some way to break him free and found a stave of iron that must have been torn away from one of the masts. I stabbed it down between the links of the chain and, leaning back, snapped them. I hurled away a rowing bench and the fellow stood.

"I'll help," he said.

"This should make it easier," said a voice behind me. Startled, I spun about. Jask stood there with an iron key. He handed it to me. "For the slaves below decks. See to them. I'll help this one free the oar-slaves. There are no keys for their chains."

I did not ask him why he helped us. "Aye," was all I said, and grasping the key tightly, I ran for the slave-hold.

I made my goal just as another big wave swept the deck clear behind me. Stumbling down the steps, I found water that came nearly to my waist. The walls bulged inward beneath the pressure of the sea, which forced a thin spray of liquid through the boards. There remained a little light, for some of the hanging lanterns had not yet gone out.

The Koro were there, neck deep in water. They had been bound with their backs to long, thick beams, the chains looped over and under the wood. In the relative quiet of the hold, their screams ripped at the ears, the fettered men wailing like blind animals. Some were dead, and vomit floated on the water where even hardened sailors had puked in terror. Around us, the whole ship shuddered and thrummed, like a harp played by the wind.

I grabbed the first man I came to and unlocked his chains, but when I tried to hand him the key he yelled wildly and ran for the stairs. I unlocked a second who, though clearly frightened, took the proffered key and began releasing those near him. Men began to beg for freedom. Tearing a stout plank from the steps, I raced across the hold. Heril was there, Teware next to him, and I shoved the board between the chains and the wooden beam and in a frenzy snapped the metal links, freeing them both.

"Good to see you!" Heril shouted, before grabbing a plank and following my example.

We moved as swiftly as we could before the ship went under, but we did not move fast enough. The gallant lady struck something in the water and the wall at our backs exploded inward. The sea ripped through, hurtling us across the hold. The beams to which the slaves were bound snapped like straw. Men shrieked as they were torn away from their chains, leaving limbs behind. The ship keeled completely over and began to come apart, like paper in the rain.

I fell and struck water, going under deeply, tumbling end over end. Objects buffeted me but eluded my grasp. I fought the ocean even as it pulled me deeper. It seemed years since I had drawn a breath. My chest burned with need. The remnants of a wall slammed into me. Then it was gone and I was thrust upward by a wave rising from beneath. My head broke the surface. A breath full of spume shuddered into my lungs.

A heavy timber struck me brutally in the side and I grabbed for it and held on. Somehow, I had been thrown clear of the ship, and what was left of that ship was dying in the surf with a spine of coral through her vitals and a gaping hole where the forward hold had been.

I lost sight of the vessel as more waves smashed me under. But I did not let go of the beam. I doubt it could have been pried from my grip. When the waves relented enough for me to regain the surface, I shook the water from my eyes and looked about desperately for some sign of other slaves.

In a flash of lightning that froze raindrops for an instant, I saw a wildly flailing shape only a few feet from me. I shoved the beam toward the figure and a thin arm caught at it and clutched. In the next stroke of lighting I saw Teware's face, gashed and bleeding but alive, across from me. A glance toward the ship showed that she was gone, broken up. She had fought well. Again, I saluted her in my thoughts.

Exhausted, Teware and I clung to our beam and let the sea push us where it willed and pound at us with its waves. Finally, my feet struck bottom, either a reef or the sloping beach of an island that lay invisible in the storm wrought darkness—or perhaps it was truly night now, for I had lost track of time. I tried to get my feet under me but the waves rolled brutally on and broke the attempt. We were shoved forward on our faces in the water, and then the sea beat to white froth around us. My knee struck something jagged and pain lanced up my leg, but my feet found purchase and I stood.

Teware still clung to the beam, too weak to gain his feet. I staggered forward, pulling him with me. A wave smashed me down. I spat out saltwater and dragged myself on all fours toward the shore. The timber that had once saved us now held us back. I abandoned it—not without a twinge of fear—and, pulling the young Koro's slack body, crawled slowly out of the sea.

After centuries I escaped the drag of the waves. Lifting Teware, I reeled up the slope of the beach toward some trees that had refused surrender to the storm. Their crowns bowed but they stood, and I hoped they would continue to stand as I lay the lad beneath their protection.

Though my legs were stone, I forced them to carry me back to the water's edge. Spray and wind and rain lashed across me and it seemed little drier on the beach than in the sea. Still, I hoped it was not my imagination telling me that the wind had died a bit and the rain had eased. The waves roared on, a beast hunting.

It seemed that nothing could survive the ocean's cauldron, but during the next few hours a dozen men washed in from the storm. Though there were Koro among them, most were oar-slaves. They had been on deck when the ship went down. The majority of the Koro had still been in the hold, and many had not been lucky enough to be thrown free as Teware and I had been.

Heril was fortunate to be among those who escaped. He crawled up on the beach not long after we did. His shoulders and back were torn and bloody, and manacles still hung at his wrists and ankles, but he carried another Koro with him. After making that one comfortable he returned to the beach and joined me in dragging men from the water.

The Green Llurn—he whom I had first freed—also rose out of the waves, like the specter of an ocean god. He carried one who must have been his friend, but the slave was dead. The Llurn's yellow eyes ran with more than rain, but he joined Heril and me after placing his friend on the sand.

After seeing the Llurn, I looked for Jask, thinking that he, too, might have survived. The Klar are much better swimmers than Humans. But I saw no sign of him, and if he lived then he must have washed up elsewhere.

At last the weather began to clear and I saw that it was indeed night, for occasional glimpses of the atmospheric shield's golden aurora flickered through breaks in the clouds. With the end of the storm came the end of my strength. I

61

managed to make it to the trees where the others lay before collapsing. I fell at once into the sleep of the near dead, a sleep without dreams.

CHAPTER SEVEN

FREEDOM AND CHAINS

In late morning I awoke, my body a mass of bruises. I rolled onto my back, groaning, and opened swollen eyes to see the golden light of the sun falling through a clear sky. Only the remnants of the storm wind played about me, tugging at my matted hair and rustling through the trees. Yet, the sea still broke harshly on the beach below us.

I heard, too, another sound besides the crash of waves. It ceased abruptly as I sat up. No doubt it was only a small animal scrounging for food. Around me lay the scattered survivors of the gale. There were at least a dozen Koro and half again that many oar-slaves, some thirty beings in all. Nearly two *hundred* slaves had been aboard the ship. I hoped other groups had survived but did not feel confident.

I stood up, though that makes it sound easy and it certainly was not. Heril stirred beside me, and the Green Llurn also awoke and got to his feet. He glanced around, his yellow eyes taking in the forest at our backs and the other sleepers who lay nearby, his nostrils flaring as he sniffed the air. He was over six feet by a whisker—just about my height—but probably weighed a lot less than I did. Of course, he had been eating only slave rations for some time. There was no fat left on him, only lean muscle, hardened at the oars.

Despite his thinness and the scars left by whips and chains, he was a magnificent specimen of his race. I knew little of them then but I learned from this one—whose name was Valyan—and from others whom I later met, the strength and courage of the Emerald Llurns, who call themselves

Nakscherii. It is a name that means "warrior people."

I have mentioned other races of Talera besides the Nak-scherii. I have told you of the Koro and the Klar, of the tiger-ish Nokarra, the avian Vhichang, and the Kaldi. There are many others. There are races who evolved naturally, such as Humans and Nokarra, and there are those who are their modified descendants, bred from other peoples as men breed strains of cattle. The Koro and the Nakscherii are examples of such. The distant ancestors of both had been Human.

There are, as well, races on Talera whose existence is the result of tampering with forces beyond Human ken, the by-products of experiments carried out by the beings who created this world. Some of these are monstrous, others beautiful. Some are much like Humans; they love, hate, cry tears of joy and of sorrow. Others seem empty. They breathe but they are empty.

I strode away from Valyan and the rest then, and went down to the beach, hoping to find more slaves who had made it to shore. There was debris aplenty, but the only bodies lay dead and swollen and stinking from the water. Sickened, I turned away. We would bury the fallen but the living were more important now.

Beneath the trees where we had sheltered, those living began to stir. Heril and I tore our clothing into rags for bandages. Valyan gathered dry wood from the heart of an old hollow log to start a fire. Few of the others seemed able to do more than roll over and groan.

I heard again the sound that had first awakened me, a scuffling that reminded me now of a stealthy boot in the dirt, and I spun on my heels in sudden realization of danger. There came a rushing, as of wind, and then a dozen and more Klar broke out of the trees wielding short staves of wood. It appeared we had washed ashore on the very beach where the Klar slavers had landed, and that they intended to recapture us.

I screamed a warning but cursed myself, knowing I should have considered this. There could not be that many islands in the vicinity. Then they hit us and my thoughts burned away in anger.

A club whistled toward my head. I caught the arm of the

beast who wielded it and threw him over my hip. He sailed through the air and crashed heavily amid the brush, but now more Klar swarmed from the trees. Most of our people were too weak and sick to fight back. They were quickly beaten senseless to the earth, leaving only the Llurn, Heril, and myself to battle on. In a quiet and savage desperation, the three of us fought, three against many.

My hand wanted a sword but the scabbard at my waist hung empty, the blade ripped away in the wrath of the storming sea. Always a practical fellow, I took a stave away from a pirate and used that.

A Klar swung at me and I blocked his stave with my own, then used the weapon like a sword to stab him in the stomach. He jackknifed with a grunt and I brought the club down on his head, the blow sounding like a shot as it struck.

Another slaver bear-hugged me from behind, knocking the stave from my grip. I strained against his strength, then snapped my arms upward to break his hold. Spinning, I clapped open palms over his small external ears. He yelped, staggered back with his hands going to his head. I kicked him in the groin and the blow hurt him badly. He retched onto the sand as he doubled over in pain.

I caught a glimpse of Valyan as he went up in the air between two attackers and smashed them back with bare feet. He moved so quickly that he seemed to flicker, his feet and the blades of his hands blurring. It looked almost like karate, of which I'd picked up a bit in the Orient. Then he disappeared into a melee of slamming bodies and flashing clubs.

Heril tripped a Klar that came for me. I caught the weapon that spun from its hands and broke the beast's jaw. Another foe charged and I put him down as well. Heril tossed a slaver over his back but slipped on a patch of wet grass and went to one knee. I was too late to block the club that took him out of the fight, but not too late to snap his attacker's arm with my own stave.

The wounded beast screamed. Yet, I lingered too long. A sound whirred in my ear—a club descending—and I ducked. That may have saved the brains from being dashed from my skull but the blow still clipped me good. I stumbled forward, barely conscious, bells clanging. A second blow struck me and I went to my knees. A last fleeting impression of despair slid through me, and then the ground rushed up and hit me in the face.

* * * * * * *

I do not like chains but I was to wear them often enough on Talera. I awoke after the fight at the trees wearing them, and yearning for lost freedom. Freedom is precious and ephemeral. Too easily it fades and is replaced by fetters, though fetters are not always made of metal. For a brief moment we had tasted liberty, but the taste was quickly gone. I was left bruised and in a foul mood, my head aching.

Since my arrival on Talera, and even before it seemed, fate had ruled me. Storms and slavers and battles had given me little chance to choose my own way. I was tired of having my life controlled by outside forces; I was mad as hell.

Someone will pay for this! I thought.

Then the incongruity of that thought struck me and I had to laugh. Here I was, in chains, my face bloody, my hair matted, my clothes little more than rags, and I was making threats. Yes, I laughed, and the other slaves looked at me as if I were insane, or as if a club had addled my wits. I merely shook my head at them, lacking the words to express what I felt, and laughed harder.

After a bit, Heril and Valyan, too, broke into laughter. We stood in our chains, roaring our mirth at the sky until the tears ran down our faces and our sides hurt. The Klar gathered around and stared. I do not truly know what made us laugh—shock perhaps, for it certainly was not bravery—but the Klar did not know that, and I think from that moment they began to doubt their hold on us. That doubt worked in our favor. Once again we were slaves of the Klar, but it was with different eyes that both the Klar and we looked on that slavery. From now on we would be watching them. And they knew it.

Still, the pirates did not fear us, and they soon came among us and began linking us into smaller coffles of ten men each. I was glad to see that a few slaves other than those in our group had survived the storm. A total of twenty-seven

Koro lived through the ordeal, along with some thirty oar-slaves—fifty-seven men out of the many who were lost.

In thinking of the horrible death that the other slaves must have experienced, chained in cold darkness as the ship came apart around them, the last of my laughter faded and a hard knot of hatred grew in my belly so that I would have killed the Klar without compunction had I been free. Yet, my hatred was tempered by the thought of Jask standing beside me on a sinking ship and handing me a key. I wondered why he had done it and what had become of him. I thought he must be dead. At least, he had not shown up in the Klar encampment, for the beasts had chosen a new captain. He shared none of the decency of Jask.

Teware had just been removed from his temporary chains when the new Klar commander walked past us. It was not he that I found of interest, however, but the small creature with brown fur and dark eyes dragging behind him on a twine leash. I started. I had not seen the creature on the ship but perhaps it had been kept below deck, or caged. I started to speak, to warn Teware to silence, but was too late.

"Behlit!" he yelled, and pulled away from his captors and started to run.

The little Toibel heard his friend's voice and rushed to the end of his leash before being jerked up short. Then the slavers caught Teware and smashed him down with their mailed fists and iron headed staves.

Heril and I leaped forward, hurling ourselves vainly against our chains. We dragged the entire coffle with us, but the whips began to fall and cut, and men cried out, and blood started bright red under the sun. I ducked my head to protect my eyes, clenching my teeth savagely. There was nothing I could do, nothing.

The Klar leader ignored the commotion and dragged the Toibel with him into one of the makeshift huts the beasts had erected near the shore. Behlit looked back and held out his hands pitifully to Teware, who lay unconscious on the sand.

CHAPTER EIGHT

INCIDENT IN THE FOREST

In the jungle sweat blooms on a man like a fungus. It leaves him stinking and slick, and cold when the wind blows. In such a jungle we found ourselves, a land choked with vines and seldom silent.

The trails we walked lay covered with fallen blooms, their scent like a rich burgundy wine. Overhead in the trees swarmed beasts akin to monkeys who hurled insults and occasionally pieces of fruit at us as we passed beneath. The air rippled with the screams and harsh calls of birds, their rainbow plumage flashing gorgeously as they preened. And sometimes in the deeper forests there came coughing growls that momentarily quieted the cacophony. It was then that I feared, for I knew the predators hunted.

The Klar did not fear the predators, for they were far more dangerous. The seventy-five or so who had survived the storm threw up an encampment on the beach not far from where their slaves had washed ashore. They built fires to smoke against the insects and to ward against the night beasts, but sometimes I saw their eyes gleaming in the darkness and wondered how far they themselves were from the savagery that haunted the jungles beyond the flames. Still, they did not seem content to stay here, and they wasted little time in putting their recaptured chattel to work. They wanted a ship, and we would build it for them.

The wreck of the Klar ship lay just offshore and the pirates salvaged much that they required, including lathes and saws and hammers, and even planks and spars. But they needed more wood and each day, before dawn, we slaves were awakened and driven in our chains up into the jungle where we felled trees amid the silver mists of morning. Teware was often with us for he had survived his beating.

The island on which the Klar ship had broken its spine was of volcanic origin and the lava cone still stood bare above the verdant growth below. The trees that carpeted the lower slopes of the island were stunted and stooped beneath their load of vines, but further up the side of the major peak we found the towering giants we sought. They grew tall and straight, with black boles and red-veined leaves.

We felled logs until the hours ran together on the mountain, and others hauled them down to the beach for final shaping. I did not envy them that job for it was on the trails below, amid the thick undergrowth, that the heat and insects took their heaviest toll. I worked most often in the high forest, and despite the fact that I was slave again, I did not despair. I would find my way free of this, and Heril and Teware would be with me.

I do not know how many days passed while we worked on the ship. It could not have been long for the vessel was still a skeleton when our situation changed. On an afternoon like all the others, I'd been given an axe and set to trimming limbs from felled trees. I watched for a chance to use the tool for something besides chopping wood, but the pirates are adept at handling men and gave me no chance. They kept our feet in close chains so that we had to mince our steps, and Klar beasts with crossbows watched us constantly.

I ignored the guards and slid into the rhythm of the axe. It moved easily in my hands; the muscles bunched and loosed on my shoulders. The soreness I had felt the first few days was gone and I was stronger than ever.

As I paused to catch my breath a rustle in the brush drew my attention. Glancing up quickly, I found myself looking into a set of pale eyes that peeked out at me from behind a berry-laden bush. It took a moment to realize that the being—of which I could see little more than a head—wore a mask daubed with swatches of green and brown that blended into the foliage around it.

Slowly, the being held up a long, human-shaped finger

69

and touched its make-believe lips, signaling me to silence. I looked carefully about, and, finding myself unwatched, nodded. It held up its finger again, then disappeared. Further up the hill a patch of brush moved against the wind. There was nothing else that day. I did not mention the incident to Heril or the others. I wasn't sure what I had seen, or what it meant. It was not long before I found out.

At dawn the next day we rose and went up the mountain again to cut trees for our masters. The morning came cooler than usual and mist clung late about the dead peak of the volcano. Toward noon the mist lifted and the sun spilled its radiance down undiluted. The Klar allowed us a break then and fed us on bits of dried fish and half of a bitter orange fruit called a tipit, which grows thickly in the jungles. The tipit tastes a little like a green persimmon to a Human—though the Klar seem to relish it—but it gives strength and one could live for some time on a diet of it.

As I finished the light meal and cast the rind away, a figure stepped into the clearing where we worked. It was a man—and by that I mean a Human—dressed in green breeches and a loose shirt of a material resembling cotton. He carried no weapons.

The newcomer was shorter and thinner than I, with close-trimmed, dark hair. His skin had a yellowish tinge to it like that of some Asian peoples, but his features were Caucasian and of a noble cast. Only the nose marred the patrician face. It had been broken in the past and had heeled crookedly. Still, I suppose he would have been called handsome, and the broken nose lent an air of rakishness to what might otherwise have been considered prettiness.

The man spoke and I understood him. In the past weeks on Talera I had acquired a working knowledge of both the Koro and Klar tongues, but he used neither of those. Yet, I understood him. He spoke quietly but his voice carried easily across the clearing, ringing with command.

The Klar did not understand the man, though, and he switched to the Koro tongue, which is a simple, straightforward language used as a lingua franca in many areas of Talera. I wondered, however, why the stranger had first spoken in English. Was he also from Earth? My pulse quickened.

"Welcome," the man said. "I am Jedik. Lay aside your weapons and remove the chains from these men, and I shall order a feast prepared."

The Klar stood tall under the splendid sunlight, their skin glistening like metal. They had no fear of a lone man, unarmed, who asked them foolishly to lay down their blades. They laughed. It was not Human laughter and there was no mirth in it, at least not as we would understand it.

The tallest of the slavers, with a double bitted war axe slung over his shoulder and a black whip that I well remembered coiled about his arm, spoke at the man. His voice echoed loud and harsh, full of arrogance.

"You have no power to welcome or deny us, Human. We are Klar. This island is ours, as are you."

"I would advise you to do as I suggest," Jedik said. "I suspected that you might prove obstinate. I did not come alone."

"Then where is your army, lout?" the Klar demanded. "Do you think us blind?"

The dark haired man smiled comfortably. He seemed completely at ease. His hands rested on his hips; his legs were slightly spread.

"You may not see them," he said, "but they hold your lives in their hands. I need only close my fist and you will die."

For the first time, the Klar leader seemed unsure. He looked around but only the verdant mass of the jungle greeted his gaze. I too looked about, but saw nothing. Not even the wind moved the trees. Yet, something nagged at me. Then, I realized what it was. The jungle lay silent, the first time I had heard it thus. The Klar did not hear the silence, or did not understand it.

"I see nothing, Human who calls himself Jedik. I think you are alone."

"That is your choice," Jedik replied. "I've warned you."

Again I glanced about the forest. All was empty. Could the man called Jedik be insane? I did not think so. I felt a faint chill, as if Death were passing by and had stopped for an instant, silently hovering.

SWORDS OF TALERA, BY CHARLES ALLEN GRAMLICH

The Klar leader acted. He drew the axe over his shoulder with one massively thewed arm and uttered his war cry in a screaming guttural. He leaped, and died with a dozen black-fletched arrows through his body. In the instant before he breathed his last he looked up at the lean form of Jedik, who had not moved.

"I thought it a bluff," he said.

"You were mistaken," Jedik replied.

I heard then the clash of weapons falling to earth, and as suddenly as that we were no longer slaves.

Men came from the jungle carrying yellow longbows nocked with steel-tipped arrows. Many of the archers were tall and straight and lean, but others were oddly bent, with distorted limbs. A few were hideous. All except Jedik wore masks that made jade and scarlet and turquoise splashes against their brown and green clothing. Many of the masks represented Human features, but some showed the faces of beasts and others could have as easily been demons.

One among the warriors was very small and wore a mask patterned in forest colors, the same mask I had seen staring at me from the bushes the day before. This one took Jedik's hand. Something made me think that it was Human, though it was no larger than a child and was malformed, with a curved back and arms longer than its legs. It ran on all fours.

The Klar were bound and marched off, and the little warrior took the key to our fetters from the dead pirate and came around to free us. When it had unlocked my chains, I spoke to it.

"Thank you," I said in English.

It started and looked up. I caught a glimpse of gray eyes, intelligent eyes. Then the being looked back at Jedik. He, too, had heard me speak and walked across the clearing to stop before me. His eyes were also gray; his gaze held both curiosity and friendliness.

"Do you understand me?" he asked in English.

"Yes," I replied.

"What is your name?"

"Ruenn Maclang," I told him. "And yours?"

"Jedik. Jedik ver lha Yed. I welcome you to our island."

"And we thank you for freeing us."

"We allow no slaves here," he said simply. "Are there more of your people?"

I looked about the clearing. There were twenty of us gathered in this place, Heril included.

"About forty," I told Jedik. "And a Toibel."

"I have seen Toibels," he said. "How many more Klar are there?"

"Over sixty."

"They are camped on the beach, I take it?"

"Yes. But they may not all be there now."

"How is it you speak English?" Jedik asked me. He pronounced it "Aihnglish."

"I was going to ask you that also."

He nodded. "Later we will speak. For now, your friends must be freed."

"Aye," I said.

The being who had unlocked our chains brought a knife and scabbarded rapier and Jedik buckled them on. I noted that he was left handed, like Teware and Valyan. I am right handed. Interestingly, left handedness is much more common among Humans of Talera than of Earth. The distribution is about half and half. This must be due to the selective nature of the population originally brought here from Earth.

Humans are, of course, not native to Talera. In fact, there are no native races on the planet. All of them—Klar, Human, Nokarra, and all the plants and animals that exist here now—originated elsewhere and were brought here by the beings who created this world. Only, it seems that most of the races arrived so long ago that there are only vague legends of other worlds and other homes.

Even had I known this at the time, it would not have explained how Jedik and his people spoke English, for the tongues brought here from Earth have long since evolved into unrecognizable forms. The answer to the riddle of Jedik would have to wait until later, until the rest of the Klar captives were free.

With thoughts of the slaves in mind, I picked up a saber dropped by one of the Klar. It was heavy but I was accustomed to swinging an axe. They are not the same thing, I will admit, but then a saber is not a weapon for finesse. Its purpose is to hack through armor and flesh as an axe hacks through wood.

"Hell waits," I muttered to myself, and we went a long way down through the jungle to the sea.

CHAPTER NINE

AN UNCARING SUN,
AN OBLIVIOUS SEA

Along our way down through the jungle to war for our friends, we slipped up on two other parties of slavers. Four Klar and a dozen slaves were taken. The latter joined us as free men and were given captured weapons. The Klar joined their brethren as prisoners.

Most of the pirates were on the beach, however, when we came to the edge of the forest and looked out secretly upon them. The majority were at work on the ship's skeleton where it lay on the sand, but there were guards who watched the trees. We could have shot those guards with bows but the rest were out of range. I said as much to Jedik.

"You're right," he said. "Our arrows would as likely strike your people as the Klar."

I wondered why he called them *my* people.

"Then it will have to be hand to hand," I said.

He did not reply but stepped out of the jungle onto the sand. The rest of us followed. There were thirty-two ex-slaves and some fifty of Jedik's men. Even the most mal-formed carried weapons, including the small being with the gray eyes who carried a sling and seemed to know it well. We were dressed in browns and greens and in the tattered clothing of slaves, but our eyes were free and clear. The masks of Jedik's men fractured the light; our weapons glinted like venom.

The guards saw us. They did not run. Their shouts brought the other Klar. There were sixty of them and more of us, but they carried iron shields and even in the heat they had left on their mail. They were slavers and I had come to hate slavers, but they were courageous for all that, courageous and arrogant.

Their commander strode toward us. On his left arm he wore a blue shield emblazoned with a silver hawk, signifying his clan membership. His men followed him, except for a few who held crossbows on the other slaves. Those would be of no help to us.

"I see you have acquired something of ours, Human," the commander said to Jedik, pointing at myself and the other ex-slaves. "For returning them to us we will let you live."

Jedik ignored his words. "I will tell you what I told your men before. Release your prisoners and lay down your weapons, and you are free to go."

"I think not," the Klar replied.

"We outnumber you," I added.

"And we are Klar," he replied.

Oh yes, they are an arrogant people. But dangerous as a razorback hog.

"What have you done with my warriors?" the being asked Jedik.

I thought him concerned for them. I was mistaken.

"They are safe in chains," Jedik told him. "All except for one who called a bluff that was not a bluff."

"When we have finished with you I shall see that they are all whipped for cowardice," the Klar said, drawing a war axe from over his shoulder. He waited, his challenge issued.

Obeying the demands of honor, Jedik's men cast aside their bows and drew their own steel. For a moment, tension ached. The saber twitched in my fist. Then, with a savage yell, Heril leaped forward, swinging a borrowed axe over his head. The beast commander caught the stroke on his shield but the blow drove him to his knees. He surged up, hurling Heril back, and lashed out with his own axe. I watched Heril leap away and then saw no more of them as the beach exploded into motion.

War cries tore the sky. Steel whistled through air and rang on steel, or thunked into soft flesh. Men screamed with the impact and went down hard. Blood clotted the sand and stained the bright swords with ugliness.

Numbers were on our side and our first charge carried them back. They recovered and held. Bodies piled up. Men stumbled over the dead and few who went down were given the chance to rise again. Axes and swords lifted and fell, came away drawing screams or soft sighs of death. Our enemies were cold and disciplined, but so too were Jedik's men, and the slaves were hot with anger. It was that passion which finally broke the Klar line. But we paid for it in blood.

The battle shattered into a dozen small melees. I made ample use of my appropriated sword. Taking up the shield of a dead Klar, I hooked it over my left arm and I killed again and again. Gore spattered me. Only a little of it was my own, spilled from a cut on the shoulder and from my arm where the dagger of a Klar beast had ripped the flesh. I opened that one's face with the saber and kicked him away from me.

I knew how to use a sword. I had learned long ago on Earth how to parry and thrust and dance around a fencing mat so that one looked good for the ladies. But there are no bodies fouling a fencing arena. There is no blood to make your footing slippery, and one wears armor for protection, not rags.

Yes, I knew how to use a sword. But it was not the same as using one in combat. I had been lucky when I'd helped Jask fight off his would-be assassins, and I was lucky again. That and the shield, and my natural quickness, were all that saved me from dying on that beach. But I never thought about luck during that battle. I thought only of my anger.

When my shield was hacked into scrap metal from the mad hammering of axes, I cast it away. I took the saber in both hands and leaped in, swinging. One blow tore away a Klar's head and the return stroke took off another's hand, leaving both stumps spouting fluid. The sun stood scintillate, uncaring in the sky. The sea rolled on oblivious. And men died.

I saw a blue shield gleaming and bashed my way toward it, but Jedik reached the Klar commander first. The pirate was good with his axe. He had wounded Heril, who had been carried off, and others of our crew had fallen beneath his steel. But Jedik mastered him easily. Never had I seen such speed and skill in the handling of a blade. The Klar leader died with a surprised look on his face and a hole through his heart where Jedik's sword had been, and gone.

Even after their captain fell, the remaining Klar fought on. It was butchery now. We surrounded them one by one and hacked them down. My anger had burned up in the war and I grew sick of the stench and sight of death. But I continued to kill. I would not leave it to others just because it was an unpleasant task, and I opened the throat of the last foe left.

Teware was among those who still remained in Klar chains, but in a few moments those links were struck off and the young Koro hurried to the hut that had been set aside for the Klar leader. He emerged moments later with an ecstatic Behlit in his arms.

Jedik's men started to gather wood and fires were soon burning. Water was boiled to tend the injured, even for the few Klar who had survived.

Jedik came over to where I knelt binding Heril's wounds.

"How is it?" the lean swordsman asked.

Heril forced a grin, though his lips stretched white with strain. "Ach, it hurts a bit," he said.

"He'll live," I said, "but will probably prove to be an insufferable patient."

"Count on it," Heril said.

We all laughed.

Jedik squatted near me. "You are skilled with a sword," he said.

"Not as skilled as you," I replied.

"You have not been trained. That is all. Later, I will show you."

I did not tell him that I had spent several years in training. My pride had taken a beating since arriving on Talera. I forced myself to swallow a bit more of it now.

"Thanks," I said. "I imagine I'll need that knowledge."

He nodded. "You most assuredly shall."

CHAPTER TEN

CITY IN THE MIST

When at last our wounds were bound and we had rested a bit, we went up the mountain through the jungle, moving very slowly for we carried the injured and the dead with us. We followed a narrow, lava-strewn trail around the curve of the volcanic peak, and there we came upon a city of purple stone where dwelt Jedik and his people. Emira it was called, Emira of the amethyst towers, a city of mists lying beneath the cone of a long extinct volcano.

The trail ran high on the mountain where we could look over much of the eastern, western, and southern portions of the island. A view of the north was cut off by the cinder cone. The eastern half of the island, where the Klar ship had wrecked, was a jungle full of sharp ravines and broken outcroppings of lava. Nothing lived there except for birds, insects and heat.

I guessed that Jedik's people spent little time in the east, and when I looked to the west I saw why. Compared to the former it was a paradise of hardwood forests and ripening fields of grain. The breeze blew much cooler there, and in the distance lay a sparkling sapphire sea, capped by white breakers. Ships rocked at anchor in that sea, their sails brilliant white, and smoke rose from huts along the shore. The jungle began again to the south, but it was not as thick and I could see occasional clearings full of grazing beasts.

Our wounded were carried on into the city but the remainder of our party climbed above the walls to where an ancient lava vent opened in the volcano's flank. We entered that vent and there, in the cool, dry atmosphere of the mountain's heart, we laid the bodies of the dead to rest and put their weapons near them. They were placed on biers of rose wood with the petals of violet and golden blooms strewn about.

Jedik spoke for them all, giving their souls to the wind, and even the Klar had prayers said over them and were gilded with flowers. There they would lie, the Klar dead and ours, until the cool stone drew the moisture from their remains. And, later, jeweled sarcophagi would be brought and the mummies put to their final rest.

From that place of tombs we went back the way we had come, feeling very old, and we sealed off the entrance to the vent with blocks of amethyst stone laid there for that purpose. Only then did the rest of us enter the city.

Constrained by the mountain out of which it was born, Emira had grown upward instead of outward like so many cities of Earth. It was small in land area but still large for its population, which appeared to number no more than a few hundred. I wondered how so few people could have constructed such a place, with its towers and spidery bridges, its fountains and the smooth dark pave of the streets.

Women watched us from terraces as we walked those streets. There were few children. I knew them only by their shapes and sizes for all wore masks. Some of the watchers turned away to be comforted by friends as they saw gaps in our lines where lovers and fathers had once strode. Others tossed flowers into the air to waft downward upon us, among them the black blooms of the nightrose, which holds death in its beauty and is a reminder of things lost.

Among the masked figures on the balconies there were subtle deformations of limbs and trunks, and sometimes not so subtle. I did not question Jedik on this for I sensed a deep pain that twisted his smile whenever he looked upon those distorted outlines. It was a pain I did not understand and into which I did not wish to intrude.

Along broad avenues of polished lava our motley band traveled, avenues that shone dark beneath the afternoon sun, and where the volcano made a northern wall for the city we came upon a crystal stream that flowed from the shaded

80

mouth of a cave. The water tasted sweet and cold. We drank our fill and then bathed in a chill pool damned up into a shallow basin for just that purpose. For the first time in weeks I felt clean and even managed to scrape away my burgeoning beard, using clear water as a mirror and a sharpened dagger for a razor.

Fresh clothing was brought. We dried ourselves on soft grasses and pulled on somber brown tunics and cloaks woven from a cloth much like cotton. Only later did I find out that it *was* cotton, the plant having been brought here from Earth.

Other Earth plants that have adapted, or been adapted, to Talera include peas, beans, onions, corn, potatoes, various kinds of berries, grapes, and such flowers as roses and lilies. Oaks, elms, maples, walnuts, and pecans make up good portions of the Taleran forests, and I later saw huge orchards of apples and pears and peaches. Taleran animals whose ancestors came from Earth include horses, dogs, elephants, many varieties of birds, honey bees, pigs, chickens, some cattle, and rabbits.

It was evening by the time we finished our ablutions. The gold had fled from the sky, leaving it a deep indigo, and the first moon was rising. There are, incidentally, four moons in Talera's sky. The first is the smallest and is a very pale blue. It has many names in the various languages of Talera but the name I prefer is Nimeru, which means, the dreamer. The remaining moons are all of different colors and each is larger than the one before. The second moon is turquoise, the third golden, and the fourth and largest is crimson. They are Sieona, the storm queen, Tisiminna, the beauty, and Rath, the warrior.

Tisiminna is circled by two smaller orbs, both of silver, and they are called the courtiers. It is said that Tisiminna was once a Human princess—or a Klar princess if you are Klar, or a Nokarran princess if you are Nokarran—and that she loved a great warrior who fell in battle. She refused to accept the loss and pined away for her love. Many courtiers tried to woo her hand but she would have nothing to do with them.

At last the gods took pity on her, for her beauty was great and her sorrow so strong, and they transformed her into

81

a moon. So that she would not be alone, the gods set two of her courtiers to circle her eternally. In other versions of the legend, Rath, the fourth moon, is the warrior that she loved and the courtiers are said to be their children.

Beneath the satiny blue light of Nimeru, we reentered the main part of Emira. Lanterns swung aloft on a delicate tracery of wrought iron bridges that connected the amethyst towers. They burned a brilliant white with the oil of the run-dal, a fish that dwells in coastal waters of Talera.

Long tables were set up in the streets where the entire population could gather, and we dined on fish, lightly braised in golden butter, and the double yoked eggs of the sea tull. Fruits from the jungle, among them the tipit, were laid out amid gloom sweetened wine-berries from the upper terraces of the mountain and potatoes, onions, and corn from the fertile slopes below the city. For dessert there was berry cobbler and grain cakes laced with honey. Throughout the meal we consumed glass after glass of rich tea, a sweet Taleran tea brewed from the leaves of the verhlis bush.

When the meal was finished, the tables were cleared by swaying women whose silver and golden masks made lovely contrasts against their blue-gray robes. The distortions beneath those robes did little to disturb their graceful movements.

From somewhere, music began to play. Lyres and flutes and a seven stringed guitar called a Kalina joined their harmonies together, the strain melancholy. The Emirians listened quietly, making no sound but their breathing.

There are no melancholy bones in Koro bodies, however. The sailors sat politely for a time, but when blood-wines loosened their tongues their own voices began to rise in song. They too took up instruments, and the music became lively and loud, and even a little raucous.

The Koro began to dance. Though the night was chilly, many threw off their cloaks and leaped on the tables to kick their feet and clap their hands. Other ex-slaves joined them, rejoicing in their freedom. Perhaps you think this unseemly when so many had died, but you must remember that the customs of the Koro are not ours. They do not love their dead less nor sorrow less than we do. They simply express

82

themselves differently. Many a poem would be composed to lost comrades later this night, and many tears would be shed, but these were private things to them and not for the eyes and ears of others.

I saw that most of the Emirians understood, though some turned away as if in pain and moved off with slumped shoulders. The others swayed silently in the torch-cast shadows and got quietly drunk.

Jedik sat somewhat aloof, and I with him. Behlit squatted on his lap and the Emirian leader fed the Toibel bits of fish. To break the silence between us I asked him about the population of the island.

"There are just over seven hundred of us here," he said. "Most are men but there are some women as well."

"I thought I did not see many children," I said.

He looked at me, his eyes boring into mine. "There are no children in Emira," he said.

"But I thought...." And then I caught myself. One foot in the mouth was enough. "Forgive me," I said.

"There is no need to apologize, Ruenn. You could not know."

He had stopped feeding Behlit for a moment and the small creature nuzzled his fingers. He smiled, a little sadly I thought, and ruffled the Toibel's fur.

"My people are sterile," he said. "You see around you only the remnant of proud men and women, their pride humbled."

In hearing him, I thought there remained a bit of pride.

He turned to me then and there was a look in his eyes as if he would seize and shake me until something fell out.

"Where are you from, Ruenn Maclang?" he asked. "I do not think it is Talera."

Carefully, I took a sip of tea. "You're right," I said. "But how did you know?"

"You speak the language of Emira."

My heart thumped. "I'm not sure I understand," I said.

"This language is spoken nowhere else on Talera."

"Yet, you speak it," I said.

"You still do not understand?"

"No."

"The language is not native to this planet."

I did not respond for a moment. When I had first heard Jedik speak in English I'd felt a surge of hope that perhaps here was another exile from Earth. I had then abandoned that thought. Though the dialect was similar his speech was not identical to the English I was familiar with, and all other signs had indicated to me that Jedik's people were natives. Hearing his words now renewed the hope I had felt.

"Are you then from Earth?" I asked him.

He frowned. "Earth! You're home, eh? No, I think we are not from the *same* world, though my planet was once called Earth. Our dialects are quite dissimilar, and, too, there are things you seem unfamiliar with that you would know had you come from our world."

Though expected, his words still brought disappointment. To cover it, I asked him: "How did *you* come here?"

"On a ship," he said. "A ship that sails the oceans between stars. And you?"

I marveled at Jedik's casual mention of crossing between the stars, but I believed him. I fear my ability to accept the extraordinary had grown of late.

"I came through something that I can only call a door," I said. "My brother was pulled in as well. I suspect he's somewhere on Talera but I don't know where."

"How long ago was this?"

"About a month and a half," I told him.

He nodded. "I knew something had happened at about that time. There were reports of many strange occurrences, of voices from the sky, and of beasts appearing unlike any that had been seen before. But I have heard nothing of another Human stranger. Perhaps you should tell me the entire story."

I did so, leaving nothing out.

"The sphere gates," he said when I finished.

"What?" I asked.

"You did indeed come through a door," he said. "They are called sphere gates. They are found on my world, and obviously on yours as well."

"What are they?" I asked.

"Passages between different realities, different universes. They were created by a race called the Selkrie, who I believe are native to my own universe. They are opened using a jewel called a milkstone, a *toir'in-or*. The milkstones are capable of amplifying mental power so that what their owner thinks about becomes reality. Or near to it. It requires training and great mental discipline."

I thought of the stone I had seen on the altar in that temple back on Earth. Had that been a milkstone?

"And your ship came through one of these sphere gates?" I asked.

"We crashed here. We probably entered this universe through such a gate but I'm not sure. I was not—uh—awake at the time."

"Your people were injured in the crash?" I asked, and instantly regretted it, thinking of the pain an earlier question of mine had aroused. However, he did not wince at my bluntness.

"Not exactly," he answered. "It's difficult to explain. I do not know how advanced your planet's technology is."

"Probably not very," I said, "since I don't know the meaning of that word."

He chuckled. "Well, you may not have the background to understand, but I will try to explain. A vast war was fought on my planet, which is called Thanos, and I and all those here in Emira took part. In fact, we were the backbone of our legions. It was necessary. And perhaps this will be the most difficult for you to grasp. It was necessary that we be available to our armies throughout the war. Those who died were recreated to fight again and again as long as they were needed."

I believe my mouth dropped open. Actually, I know it did. All the strangeness I had seen and heard had not prepared me for this—people being brought back from the dead!

"How is such possible?" I asked in amazement.

"The procedure is called cloning," he said. "You see, each bit of tissue in our bodies, our skin and hair, everything, contains a copy of the map by which we are built. When that map is unraveled the entire person can be regrown from a single small piece. I am told the procedures are not difficult when one has the knowledge, though I'm afraid I lack it.

"Before the war, small scrapings of our skin were taken and frozen to preserve them. Our memories and emotions were stored away in sophisticated machines that have many similarities to living beings. They are called computers. If any of us died then the computers were activated and new bodies grown. The memories were returned to the bodies and we were as before. The clones were never exactly the same as the original but they had much the same skill at war. It was a major reason for our victory."

He looked at me, I suppose to see if I still followed his words. I merely stared at him.

"I know it is difficult to understand," he said, "but it is true nevertheless. When the war ended we asked that the cloning tissues and computers be destroyed so that we could live out normal lives. We were told that they were. But the devices were located on great ships that circled our planet and at least one of those ships survived. It crashed here on this island, to the north of the peak, and the computers were activated. They began to recreate the stored clones but were themselves damaged in the crash. I was first to be reborn and am the most nearly complete. But even I am sterile.

"The computers became increasingly erratic over time. The early clones were only mildly affected. The later ones were hideously deformed. I tried to stop the machines but they had their own defenses and would allow no one near them. Eventually, they simply ran down.

"Almost two thousand clones were made, many so incomplete that they could not survive. Some died quickly; others lingered for weeks, constantly in pain. About a thousand of us lived. All suffer some handicaps. My people wear masks because they lack facial features and hair. Those whom you thought were children are only the ones who are most distorted, or those who have no legs."

"And some of them are *your* clones," I said, guessing it and aching for him.

"Yes, many of them. There were about a dozen originals stored in the ship's computers. All those you see here are versions of those few patterns."

He stopped then, as if his tale was complete, but after a time he picked up the story again in a very quiet voice.

"We struggled to survive that first year and many failed. But in time we built Emira and began to grow enough food to support ourselves. There were machines aboard the ship to help with that. We constructed our own vessels to explore the nearby seas and we began to trade with other cultures. None of them know the truth about us. We have been here nearly a hundred years. Some have died during that time but slowly we have built up this island and made it a home."

He looked at me again. "How old do you think I am, Ruenn?"

"You don't look quite a hundred," I said dryly.

He smiled. "And I won't for a long time. On Talera, men age very slowly. Something in the air, perhaps. Or the food. Some men are said not to age at all." He smiled more broadly. "You are very young now, Ruenn. I do not know how long people normally live here but you may have several hundred years ahead of you."

I returned his smile with a sickly one of my own. There was too much to understand, and I could not imagine living a *hundred* years, let alone several hundred.

He laughed aloud and slapped me on the shoulder. His melancholy mood seemed to have melted away, as if telling me his story had relieved some of his pain.

"Come, let me show you Emira," he said.

I rose and went with him. We walked the empty streets until the music faded behind us. The second and third moons—Sieona and Tisiminna—had risen. Their green and gold light contrasted with the blue of Nimeru and with the purple stone of which the city was built, and the landscape loomed eerie and beautiful beneath the moons' shine. We walked a good distance and at last stopped on a feathery bridge that extended between two terraces. Leaning on the railing there, the city of Emira lay unfolded beneath us.

"How much do you know of Talera?" Jedik asked me.

"Not much," I admitted. "But I'm willing to learn."

He turned his back to the railing and looked up at the two moons in the sky. "Talera." He said it very carefully, almost lovingly. "I have always liked that name. I will tell you as much as I have learned of this world, but there is much I do not know as well."

"Anything would be of help."

"Yes, of course," he said. "Well, to begin with you may have realized that this planet is not natural."

I nodded.

"The beings who created it are called the Asadhie. No one knows what they look like, though legends have it that they can assume the shapes of men or of other beings and that they often travel about the world in such guises. It is also said that they find much enjoyment out of raising and destroying civilizations at a whim, or as if it were some great game they are playing. I wonder sometimes if the legends are true. Talera's history is so chaotic that it certainly seems as if the problems are being deliberately caused.

"Anyway, it is said that the Asadhie condensed Talera out of the heart of a giant, gaseous planet. The remnants of the gas still surround us and a shield was placed in the atmosphere to hold it back. This is the aurora you see at night. The sun and the moons were set below the shield. I do not know how it is that they seem to act as a normal sun and as normal moons do, but I suppose it was not difficult for the Asadhie. The sphere gates were used to bring plants and animals and intelligent beings from many worlds here to populate their creation. From what you told me, those gates still work on some worlds and may still be used to bring beings here, perhaps as slaves."

"Do you think the Klar slavers might be the ones who took Bryce and my men then?" I asked.

"It was not a Klar who opened the gate on your world. The being that you described was a Thye Vessoth, a wizard race created artificially by the Asadhie. However, it is possible that your people ended up in Klar hands. There have long been rumors of dealings between the Thye Vessoth and the Klar."

"Then I must go to the slaver's hold," I said. "I have no other place to look. And if there is any chance of finding my brother I must take it."

"I understand," he said. "Only, wait until your men have healed, and mine as well, and we will accompany you."

"That is not necessary. It's not your fight."

"You'll need a ship," he said. "I have one. Besides, it is

time for the Klar to learn that they cannot make slaves of men with impunity."

"Very well then," I said. "You and your warriors will be welcome."

I held out my hand to him and he took it. Over his shoulder the fourth moon was rising, its color like blood over the towers.

CHAPTER ELEVEN

ON THE MOUNTAIN

The days in Emira are melancholy, the nights seductive. We passed a week and then two in the city while those wounded in the battle with the Klar healed. I spent some of that time with Jedik but even more of it alone on the mountain, letting the silence enter my soul. The lorn wind blew about the volcanic peak, playing dirges in the empty lava funnels. Both beauty and pain lived in that wind, and the drifting ghosts of ancient memories.

Following the wind, I found the place where the Emirians' star ship had crashed. Broken fingers of metal stabbed at the sky; the portals and open doors were like eye-less sockets. Yet even after a hundred years no rust fouled that steel. It lay as it had lain on the day it met its end.

Often when on the mountain, I sat on a smooth chunk of porphyry that had been quarried for the city's walls but never used and looked down from the heights into the ways of Emira. I watched the quiet people pass along the lava streets and saw them drink their dark wines amid hanging terraces full of scarlet and golden flowers. I saw them wend their way to assignations on the spidery bridges and watched them touch and hold each other but never kiss.

And near that rock, in a silence-stroked hollow overhung by a massive cliff, I found where the dead heroes of Thanos had been laid to their final rest in sarcophagi of violet stone. On the coffin lids were carved the physiognomies of noble men and women, the features of those within as they had been in their lives before the accident of Talera. When I touched those stone faces they seemed wet with purple tears.

On a day when I sat in that place, wrapped in a gray cloak against the chill that clung to the mountain even in the summer, Heril Rolvfshern came to me. His face was drawn and white but no blood stained his bandages. It seemed that his wounds were largely healed.

I sheathed the sword that rested in my hand. It was a long, slender rapier with a straight, single edged blade that was exquisitely balanced. Jedik had given it to me to replace the saber I had taken from the Klar, and we had practiced long hours together in a small amphitheater that had been dusted with sand. I was much better with a blade now than I had ever been before.

I sheathed the sword and looked at Heril.

"We have been searching for you," he said.

Valyan, and Teware, and a number of others stood behind him.

"I was watching the clouds," I said.

"And thinking of home, perhaps?"

"Yes, that too," I agreed.

I had told Heril my story over a chalice of wine, feeling the need at first to explain why I had been free aboard the Klar pirate ship while he and the others had been chained in the hold. One revelation led to another and soon I had spoken to him of Earth. He had not seemed particularly surprised.

There is a saying among those on Talera who know of the gates between worlds that: "All sphere gates lead to Talera." Though rare, it is apparently not unheard of for strangers to arrive on the planet from far worlds. In fact, Jedik suggested to me that some Talerans occasionally seek out such strangers, as slaves or warriors, or perhaps for other purposes.

Heril was aware of this. The Koro are not particularly well educated as Talerans go but Heril was an exception to the rule. He had told me that his mother was considered something of a scholar among his people, although he himself had followed more in the tradition of his father. I looked at him now, with the wind ruffling the fur collar of his cloak against his blond beard, and saw that there was something he

91

wanted to say.

"What is it you wish to speak with me about?" I asked him.

"I...uh...we." He lifted a hand to indicate those who stood behind him. "We wondered if you might ask Jedik for permission. And perhaps for the use of tools. So that we could finish work on the ship we were building for the Klar."

"For what reason," I asked, though I was sure that I knew.

"We Koro would go in search of our people who were taken by the Klar," he said.

"And many of those who were oar-slaves desire to go for similar reasons," Valyan added. "I myself have friends who are still slaves. I would not wish to leave them to the loving care of the Klar."

I nodded to them. It was as I had thought.

"I have already spoken to Jedik and there will be no need to work on the Klar ship," I told them then. "The Emirians have graciously offered us the use of one of their vessels. And, of course, I wish to accompany you. If my brother is on Talera he will be unfamiliar with its ways. It is quite possible that he may end up a slave."

Too, I was thinking of my cousin, Eric Ryall, and the others of my crew on Earth who had disappeared the same night that I had been transported to Talera. And yet another face churned in my memories, as well, a woman's pale face framed by dark hair. Even her scent seemed always with me, and Rannon had been her name. My knuckles whitened on the pommel of the sheathed sword.

Heril bowed slightly at my words. He seemed relieved. Yet, there was clearly something else he wanted to say.

"What is it?" I prompted him.

He scuffed his boot on the stone, then looked up and fixed me with his glance. "We hoped that you would lead us," he said.

I was startled.

"Why?" I asked him.

"You have the Khi," he said.

I knew enough of the Koro language to know what Khi meant. There is no exact equivalent in English but it means—among other things—presence, power, charisma, spirit. It is a term commonly used to describe those who are natural leaders of men. Heril had done me great honor.

"But I am not even of your world," I protested.

"Khi knows no ancestry," Valyan said. This, too, is a saying of Talera.

"I am not good enough," I said.

"You will be," Heril replied.

He walked forward and the others followed. Swords were unsheathed, axes drawn over shoulders. One at a time the men touched a knee to the mountain and laid their weapons at my feet. I stood there, rigid, but did not object for that would have dishonored them. A chill coursed the length of my spine. I did not think that I was worthy. I had led men before but never in such an undertaking as now faced us. No, I was not worthy, but—as Heril had said—I would be. I would have to be.

When each man had come forward and stepped away again there were twenty weapons on the stone at my boots. Twenty men stood before me. As suddenly as that I became responsible for their lives. I picked up the weapons one by one and handed each back to the warrior who claimed it.

Heril was last to come forward. "*Hai Khisan,*" he said, which means, literally, "honor to he who leads by the force of will." In English it would perhaps be rendered as, "Warlord."

I gripped my friend's shoulder. "I will need your help," I told him.

He nodded, and we turned and went down the mountain to Emira.

CHAPTER TWELVE

DARK WARRIOR

We did not leave the city immediately. There were plans to be laid, food to be stocked for the long voyage, and we had also run quickly into an unforeseen snare. I had assumed that Valyan or some other oar-slave would know where the Klar homeland lay. I was mistaken. The slavers, perhaps with good reason, seemed to wish the location of their hold kept secret and all slaves were blindfolded until well away from port. They knew the place was an island and that it hid somewhere to the south but, as Jedik quickly pointed out, the southern seas are quite vast.

"However," Jedik added, "there is one here who may know how to find the Klar."

"Who is he?" I asked, anxious to speak with him.

"He is not Emirian," Jedik said, who had fallen into the habit of explaining things to me since he knew that I was only recently come to Talera. "He is not even Human," he continued, "but a Vlih. He was once slave of the Klar and escaped. He washed ashore here in a small boat, half dead from exposure and hunger.

"He recovered quickly but has dwelt here ever since. He does not seem to wish to return to his home. Nor will he speak of that home. I suspect it is something to do with his bond group. The Vlih are fierce warriors who generally fight in small, all male groups called Vlih NHa. It is believed that all Vlih NHa are kin and that they are lovers as well. Their loyalty to each other is certainly fanatical and for a Vlih warrior to lose his bond group is the same as losing his soul.

94

Many do not survive it."

"What is this fellow's name?" I inquired.

"He calls himself Rhandh, though that is only a use-name. The Vlih do not reveal their true names to outsiders. This one dwells alone on the southern tip of the island."

"Can we find him?"

"The trouble will not lie in finding him but in persuading him to tell you what you wish to know. I believe the fellow suffers much pain and guilt over the loss of his Vlih NHa, or for some similar reason. He does not like company."

"Yet, we must talk with him," I said.

"Yes," Jedik agreed. "Come, I will show you where he lives."

A dhaur's walk (about seventy-eight minutes) through scattered woods took us to the southern end of the isle. We could have taken a boat but Jedik felt that a foot approach would be less threatening to the Vlih. Too, the fellow would not be able to see us coming and avoid us.

The trails ran clear for much of the way, worn out by the hooves of swine and cattle, the cattle being of a sturdy breed called the terval, which the Emirians herd. I was surprised, though perhaps should not have been, to see that most of the trees around us were hickories and oaks. We walked on a carpet of crackling acorns and sometimes had to push the pigs from our path as they fed on the largesse.

Only as we neared our destination did the woods became thicker, and strange with twisted, yellow trees and arm-thick vines that must be chopped aside. Here we had to make our own paths, for, as Jedik explained, the Emirians seldom visited this area.

It was not long, however, before we broke through the burgeoning jungle and came out onto a jutting, rocky promontory where little grew. The Vlih warrior was there, as we had hoped. He bent over a smoking fire on the beach, pitching the bottom of a bark canoe. He stood up as we approached and did not seem pleased. Beyond him lay a hut, its interior dark. I thought for a moment that a shadow moved there, then realized it must only be the bright sun in my eyes after the gloom of the forest. I looked back at the Vlih as we strode up to him.

He was a taller being than I, and heavier by about forty pounds, I guessed. His facial features and body pattern were largely Human, though there was something odd about his hips for he walked leaning forward. This gave him the appearance of stalking stiffly, like a wolf about to meet an enemy in combat.

The Vlih's eyes flamed like a wolf's as well, and his ears were large and slightly pointed at the tips. His hair grew black and coarse. It was cut short in the front and at the sides, and hung in a long mane down his back. His skin was very dark, and shiny with sweat. He possessed only two legs and two arms, but two thick tentacles, as long as his arms, extended from midway between his true arms and his waist. A tail flicked behind him, much like that of a hunting cat except for its lack of hair. There was something vaguely satanic about his appearance, and the stink of the burning pitch at his back did not help dispel that image.

It is said that the Vlih are marvelous fighters, adept with swords and axes and bows. There are weapons made that can be attached to their tentacles and they often go into battle with razor sharp steel strapped to their prehensile tails. This, and the fact that they seldom fight alone, makes them among the most dangerous and most feared opponents on Talera. This one, this Rhandh, carried no weapons, though I saw the scars on his body of one who had used them. And his look was weapon enough to let us know his unhappiness at being disturbed.

"What do you want, Jedik?" he asked, before we had a chance to speak. "I thought we had agreed that you would not disturb me."

"I am sorry to do so," Jedik replied. "I would not have unless it were of great importance."

"Then make it quick," Rhandh said. "I have much work to do."

Jedik waved a hand at me, and at Heril and the few others who had accompanied us.

"These men were enslaved by the Klar," he said. "They are now free but many of their friends are still imprisoned in the slaver's homeland. They wish to rescue them but do not know how to find the Klar hold. Nor do I. I thought, perhaps, that you might have the knowledge they seek."

"And you wish me to give it to you?"

"Or show us," I said.

He looked at me. His eyes held mine for a moment. Then he looked away as if dismissing me as insignificant.

His gaze turned back to Jedik. "They are fools to seek the Klar. They will end up slaves again. It is what the Klar do and they are very good at it."

"We must take that chance." I said.

Again he looked at me. He appeared angry that I dared to interrupt. I found myself growing a bit irritated with him.

"Perhaps *you* must," he said. "I owe nothing to you or these others."

"Who do you owe?" I asked him.

Jedik shook his head slightly. I ignored that warning, focused my energies only on the Vlih.

The dark warrior stalked up to me. His gaze bruised across mine.

"I am Rhandh," he said. "Who are you?"

"Ruenn Maclang."

"You have a very loud mouth, Ruenn Maclang."

"Perhaps," I admitted.

"What if I close it for you?"

"You are welcome to try. *After* we have freed our people. Until then, do not waste my time."

My arrogance surprised me. It appeared to surprise him as well. But I had spoken the truth. We had already wasted too much time. It seemed clear that he would not accompany us simply at our request. Yet, I sensed something in this one. There was pain, but there was something else as well. It felt like honor. I thought that if I could break through his facade of anger we might gain a powerful ally.

For a moment, though, I feared I had gone too far and he would attack me. His stare screeched into mine. His fists clenched and the tentacles at his sides twitched. He was taller than I, and heavier. I did not know if I could take him but was prepared to try. Perhaps fortunately, I did not have to find out. He withheld himself, with difficulty I thought. I was not sure why.

"I do not wish to fight you," he said. "Leave me."

He turned away, striving hard it seemed to maintain the arrogant cast of his shoulders. That made it harder to say what must be said.

"It is claimed that he who has lost his honor can only recoup it with an act of great sacrifice."

I spoke loudly, hating the words even as I knew that I must speak them. The lives of many men depended on this warrior, and, again, the image of a pale face and long dark hair slid through my mind.

Rannon, I thought.

The Vlih flinched at my voice, struck as if with blows. Eyes flashing, he whirled, hands rising like a raptor's talons. It seemed sure that he would attack me, but he did not. His gaze held mine, slowly losing its fire. Then he looked away and I knew that I had struck close to the heart of him. His shoulders slumped and I cursed myself.

Rhandh raised his hands to his face. His voice came from between them, low and full of hurt. "I cannot do what you ask of me," he said. "The sea was vast and I was lost in delirium for much of the last part of the journey."

His shoulders slumped further and I sensed that he felt this, also, to be a failure. I marveled at the demands he must have placed on himself. No wonder he had failed. I did not show him pity, however. Though deserving it, he would not have accepted it and I would have hurt him all the more.

"We have those among us who can bring a ship to the general area of the Klar hold," I said. "It is only from there that we would need your help. None of our people have actually seen the place from the sea."

He looked up. His eyes searched mine. "I was aware at the first," he said.

"We leave Emira with the dawn three days hence," I said. "You may join us at the harbor before that time. You will be welcome."

I then strode away and the others followed. It seemed odd that I led, for great warriors walked among them.

Jedik spoke to me once we entered the jungle. "You are steel, Ruenn Maclang. Yet, I think that you know men."

"Let us hope so," I said. "This one we need."

Chapter Thirteen

Sea Demon

In three days time we left Jedik's isle. Rhandh the Vlih accompanied us.

The sun dawned golden on that day and the soft winds of a summer morning filled our sails and drove us swiftly dancing over the wild blue sea. We rode a quicksilver craft called the Darkling, which carried twin lateen sails of white to catch the breeze, and a single row of oars in case of becalming. We did not need the oars that first morning, nor for many days after. The Darkling seemed a mare pent too long in a stall, and she raced across the waves, casting the sapphire waters back from her prow.

Rhandh, it seemed, remembered more of his journey to freedom than he had thought. He spent many hours at the helmsman's side, examining readings and charts and pointing out the direction we must take. He used the sun as guide during the day, and the moons at night, and sometimes the lighter blue of the ocean currents, which are not stained as darkly with minerals as the remainder of the sea. The Emirians supplied him with machines akin to sextants and astrolabes, and they were skilled sailors. Swiftly and smoothly they brought us onto whatever course Rhandh indicated, and we danced madly on toward the destiny that we all felt awaited us.

I was happy Rhandh had joined us. I had not been particularly surprised. I was, however, surprised to see who he brought with him in chains on the day that we sailed.

"So you survived!" I had said to that prisoner.

"Of course. Did you think I would die so easily?"

"You know this Klar?" Rhandh had demanded.

"Yes. He saved the lives of many of the slaves when the pirate ship went down in the storm."

Both Rhandh and Jedik looked at me incredulously. "A Klar!" they said in unison.

I smiled at their expressions.

Jask shrugged his shoulders. "A sudden compulsion," he said. "I think the storm had temporarily addled my wits."

"It is well that I did not kill him then," Rhandh said dryly as he stalked away.

"Yes," Jask said, loudly enough for the Vlih to hear. "He was a superb host." Then he smiled.

"I wouldn't bait him," I told the pirate.

"Nor would I," Jask agreed.

I had convinced Jedik to bring the Klar captain along, ostensibly as a hostage. I had a hunch he might prove more useful to us than that.

"I will not help you hurt my people," he had stated.

"We would not expect it," I told him.

"Very well then, I will accompany you."

I had been forced to laugh at that.

Now, a week out to sea, the tall warrior stood beside me at the rail of the Darkling, spume glistening on his scales. He was no longer chained but had been given no weapons. He asked me why, truly, I had brought him along.

"To frighten the girls," I joked with him. "Then they'll need me to comfort them."

"Humph," he replied. "A Klar female would not know whether to eat you or stake you in the garden to scare away the vulls."

I just grinned at him. "Really, I have very little idea why I brought you along. It was an impulse."

He nodded. "I thought as much."

"How did you end up a prisoner of the Vlih?" I asked him.

"When the ship broke up I was thrown into the water. There was a plank for a while but it got caught in a current that almost washed me out to sea. I had to swim for the island and by the time I made it I was so exhausted I fell asleep on the beach. It was the Vlih who woke me. With a spear. He set me to chopping firewood and gathering stones for some wall he was building. I was shut in the hut as punishment on the day you came to visit, chained rather unceremoniously and gagged. I thought he would kill me after that but he did not."

"He hates the Klar," I said. "He was once slave of your people and has not forgotten it."

"Many people hate the Klar," he said, shrugging.

"Perhaps your race should reconsider the taking of slaves, then. Or do you enjoy being so intensely loathed?"

"It is part of who we are. Though," he paused as if to study the clouds, "there are some who might wish it different."

I did not press Jask on his words and for a long time after that we remained silent. I suppose I did not really know *how* to press him. He was an enigma to me. Aboard his ship he'd seemed largely indifferent to the plight of the slaves. Oh, he had seen to it that they were well fed, but I had figured that was just his greed for the gold that healthy slaves would bring. At other times, as when the ship went down in the storm, he had seemed greatly concerned, even to the point of risking his own life to save some of theirs.

I thought there was a war going on inside of Jask, between the part of him that was a Klar slaver and the part that was capable of imagining life under the whip. Perhaps it was because he came from a segment of Klar society that had few rights and wielded little power. The clanless among the Klar, the Keshaki is what Jask had called them—and called himself—had much in common with slaves.

I put aside these thoughts after a while—not sure how they helped me better understand the pirate captain—and spoke to him once more in a lighter mood.

"Why did the Vlih have you gagged?" I asked him.

He chuckled. "He did not care for my speech."

"In other words, you talked too much," I said.

"Undoubtedly."

We laughed together there for a while, until Valyan came to fetch us for the evening meal.

Our passage across the southern sea of Talera, which is

called Trevassa, continued smoothly and the crew had time on its hands. We spent most of that time honing our skills with weapons. My swordsmanship had improved vastly since coming to Talera, but when Jedik fenced, with Valyan or with his men, and the blades leaped and danced and sent splinters of golden light flying, I could do little more than watch in awe and know that I might soon have need of such skills. I was afraid I'd be found lacking, and now others besides myself might depend on my abilities. There were those aboard this ship who meant to follow me. I could not let them down. I worked and worked until my hands blistered and I half drowned in sweat. Then I worked some more.

Eight days out of Emira the wind died. The oars were shoved out through the ports; the drums beat; the cadence sounded; and the ship was warped along by the power of muscle. The Darkling carried sixteen, extra-long oars to a side, each manned by three rowers, which is more efficient than having many smaller oars manned by one person at a time. Some of the rowers had once pulled oars on the Klar longship. Then, they had worn chains. Now, they pulled as free beings. I took my turn along with them and soon discovered new muscles that had only recently developed. Certainly, I had never known of them before.

On the second day of calm I spent my time at the oars in the morning, and in the evening worked the soreness from my back and shoulders in swordplay with Jedik. Today I seemed to have the knack. We leaped and danced about, the swords clattering together like bells.

"Good," Jedik said. "Good. But watch the overhand."

I watched it, and parried it, and my flashing blade, tipped with cork, tapped lightly along Jedik's ribs. The Emirian beamed at me as a father might when his son bests him at chess.

"Well done, Ruenn," he said.

He clapped me on the shoulder, and the deck reared up beneath us, heaving like a drunken sailor. Jedik stumbled into me and I caught him to keep us both from falling. A roaring bellow tore the air, followed by a rippling scream of pure terror. Quite suddenly, pain joined terror in that scream.

It took a moment to localize the sound as coming from

the stern, and we staggered in that direction, stumbling as the ship bucked and heaved like a living thing beneath us. Once past the stern cabins we could see clear to the aft rail. It was draped over with a mass of gray flesh, thick with writhing tentacles as wide as a man's torso. Jedik's face went white.

"What is it?" I shouted, my words barely audible over the monster's bellow and the screech of splintering wood.

"A Cenboth!" Jedik shouted back. "By the blood of Dhiez, a Cenboth!"

This Cenboth seemed a composite of all the nightmares of my youth. Its head reared up well over the ship, a fleshy bulk humped like the domed skull of a sperm whale. Platter size eyes sat widely apart on the massive face, protected by thick flaps of horny tissue that arched over them. Beneath the eyes, a gnashing beak similar to a parrot's was filled with scissor teeth. To either side of the mouth a dozen tentacles whipped the air. The bulk of the creature extended beneath the sea but I caught sight of its gigantic tail, which curled like that of a lobster as it lashed the blue water to foam.

The ship reared again as the beast shifted its bulk further up the stern. A crewman staggered and lost his balance, falling into the nest of tentacles beneath the mouth. One grabbed him and jerked him up. He had time for one long scream before the parrot beak ripped him to shreds.

"The thing will capsize the boat," Jedik shouted. "We've got to get rid of it."

The sword with which I had been practicing still hung in my fist. Quickly, I tore loose the cork guarding the tip and edge and rushed to the attack. Jedik joined me, stopping only to call for archers. I cut down at a tentacle and felt the steel bite deep. The Cenboth's skin was tough as leather but beneath the dermis the flesh was soft. It bled pink serum but the blow didn't seem to disturb the beast at all.

Another tentacle lashed overhead. I chopped up at it and the pale tip went flying off to splash in the sea. This time the creature bellowed. Perhaps the tips of the tentacles were more sensitive than the lengths. I struck at another and cut it through. Other sailors leaped to join Jedik and I. Swords and axes turned the sun as they hewed down. A lance or two went deep.

Jask grabbed an axe from the hands of a stunned crew-man and ran forward, swinging. He chopped through one tentacle but was struck by a second and hurled from his feet. In an instant he leaped up and attacked again, but our combined efforts only enraged the beast further.

Suddenly, men raced up from below decks with bows. A dozen of them drew strings and loosed. The monster sprouted arrows like a pin cushion. Most had been aimed at the eyes, but the Cenboth moved its head so erratically that many arrows missed completely. Others stuck in or glanced harmlessly away from the fleshy brow ridges that protected its vision.

Nature gives animals protection for its most vulnerable parts, I thought. It might be behind those eyes that the brain lived. Shifting my sword from right hand to left, I drew my dagger and rushed in. At the last second I hurled the knife and dodged away. Still, a tentacle struck me across the back and knocked me to the deck on my face. Heril hauled me clear of the thing's reach. The dagger had missed, striking into the pads over the eyes. Even as we watched, it fell out to clatter on the ship's planking.

The Cenboth shifted its bulk again, inching forward. Heril had to grab my arm to keep me from sliding down into the beast's maw. Our ship was dying under the monster's weight. Men died as well, crushed and smashed by tentacles or torn to rags by beak and teeth.

"Give me your dagger!" I shouted at Heril.

He handed it over reluctantly, knowing what I intended to try. I took a deep breath to calm my fears and then ran forward, ducking and dodging tentacles before hurling the dagger up into the beast's face. Instantly, I slammed the sword back into my right hand. The knife went true, into the heart of the eye where it stabbed to the hilt. The Darkling staggered as the Cenboth screeched and rocked backward.

I slipped in a pool of blood and fell. A tentacle wrapped about me and jerked me aloft. The tight coils locked the sword to my side, leaving the weapon useless. Only my left hand was free and it was empty. The world tilted sickeningly around me, blue water, gold sky, torn ship wallowing in the sea, yelling men with gore-stained weapons in their fists.

The monster drew me down toward its beak. Its good eye glittered a pale blue as it stared into mine. There was a mesmeric quality to its gaze. A shout brought my head around. I looked for a moment at seemingly distant warriors hacking madly at the creature's body. The tentacle tightened about me. I glanced back into the mouth as it opened and felt the blood roaring in my ears. It was difficult to breath through the Cenboth's restraining coils.

Again, I heard a shout and looked. Jask stood by himself near the rail, an axe shining like a torch in his hand. He saw my glance, flashed a quick smile, and then threw the axe at me. It was a perfect throw. The handle slapped solidly into the palm of my free hand.

The creature brought me down, opening its beak almost delicately. I lashed a backhand blow at the face and the axe head went in below the Cenboth's remaining eye and gashed upward. The eye popped, spattering me with a stinking, pus-colored ichor, but I followed through with the blow, burying the weapon deep in the thing's brain. The Cenboth screamed, almost like a Human, and reared in agony. Its tentacles tightened convulsively, half crushing the life from me, then abruptly relaxed.

I fell, struck the deck hard and nearly went over the side. Valyan's strong hands caught me and pulled me to safety. The ship bucked a last time, then righted itself as the Cenboth slipped backward into the sea. Men went carefully to the smashed railing, bows drawn and steel lifted, but there was nothing on the surface save pink froth. The tension leaked slowly away and the sailors gathered about and slapped me on the back. Laughter, shrill from raw nerves, sparked through the crowd.

"You saved us, Ruenn!" Jedik said to me. "Fetch him wine!" he shouted to a nearby crewman.

"I need no reward for being clumsy," I said. "Besides, it was Jask's quick thinking that truly saved us."

Most of them realized the truth of my statement and looked around at the pirate with newborn respect. Jask stood quietly.

Jedik strode over to the Klar. "Yes," he said. "We owe you. When our people are regained, you too will receive your freedom. In the meantime, you have our gratitude."

Lord Jask the Klar smiled.

"I also owe you thanks," I said.

Again Jask smiled. "That evens my debt," he said. "For the assassins."

A bottle of wine was thrust into each of our hands and we drank, deeply. Jedik did not drink with us but fell to assessing the damage caused by the Cenboth's attack. Little structural harm had actually been done to the ship. The aft railing was battered into kindling and a number of planks had been warped, nothing too serious to fix. The ship had been solidly built and it took only a few dhorrin to effect some repairs.

The loss of four crewmen, all Emirians, could *not* be repaired. I ached for their families. I ached for Jedik, who felt the loss of each of his people so keenly. He had their remains wrapped in shrouds and followed them below. I did not see him again that evening.

While we waited for the ship to get under way, the dead Cenboth floated to the surface. Torpedo shapes filled the water about it, feeding in a frenzy. Other dark forms struggled feebly in the water. They were not predators.

"Ah," Jask said. "I see now why the beast attacked us."

"Why," I asked.

"You see the small wriggling shapes about the creature's tail?"

I nodded.

"Those are its young. The Cenboth normally lives very deep in the sea. It only comes to the surface when giving birth. The little ones cannot take the pressure at the depths where the mother dwells. The beast is most ferocious when it thinks it's protecting its brood. It probably saw us as a threat."

Some of the archers had gone to the rail to shoot the offspring. They first tied strings to their arrows, to save them I supposed.

"Must they kill the babies?" I asked Jask.

"Little ones grow up," he said. "Besides," he motioned toward one of the archers who dragged a squirming young Cenboth over the ship's side, "they are quite good eating."

I shook my head, not feeling very hungry at the moment.

Shortly thereafter, the wind began to blow and we soon put the scene behind us. I was happy to see the place fall astern. Death had left its mark there.

CHAPTER FOURTEEN

ISLAND OF THE KLAR

A fish leaped in the dawn, and another, their scales catching and breaking the light into glistening, rainbow jewels. Each of the creatures stretched over forty feet long, their muscular bodies rippling with power. They were of a species called vimen and are the largest true fish of Talera. Their flesh is considered a delicacy, probably because they are difficult to catch.

Beyond where the vimen crashed back to the sea a low mist coiled on the waves. Vulls and terthins hunted baitfish near us, and when successful flew off toward that mist with raucous cries that spoke to us of land. Rhandh said that the rising vapor marked the island hold of the Klar.

We stayed well away from that island during the day and kept our sails furled. The watch saw few Klar vessels but there may have been more; the violet sails and ebony hulls of their ships are difficult to detect against the dark ocean. We also had to be sure that we ourselves were not seen. The Darkling was faster than any Klar pirate ship but only so long as the wind held, and that wind had gusted fitfully for the past few days, spending its effort in piling up gray clouds to our south.

The clouds rolled toward us and by mid-afternoon they covered the sky. The wind gusted more strongly and a fine drizzle began to drift across us. I did not think we'd get a storm but there was likely to be more rain.

Night came early beneath the clouds and no moons could be seen. We put up our sails and went swiftly in toward the low shore. The island that lay there was situated along the same great geologic rift as Jedik's Isle. It, too, was volcanic in origin, though both volcanoes had been dormant for centuries.

Unlike at Emira, the cinder cone no longer existed here. Sometime in the distant past an eruption had blown away much of the peak, and the hub of land that remained was just a memory of a greater island. Only part of the outer rim of the volcano remained, like half of a melon rind. The sea had poured in to quench the last fires, leaving a still lagoon surrounded on three sides by rock. We slid quietly past that harbor, where the black silhouettes of ships lay peacefully at anchor.

"The Klar homeland," I murmured.

"No," said Rhandh, who stood beside me.

I turned on him, startled. "What do you mean?" I demanded.

Jedik, too, eyed him questioningly. "Yes," he said. "I think you should explain yourself."

"You see this island," the Vlih said, "where the Klar ships are at anchor, and you think it is their homeland. That is what you are intended to think."

"You told us this morning when we first saw the mist that the slaver's hold was here," I said. "Have you then lied to us?"

"The homeland is here," Rhandh replied.

"You speak in riddles," Jedik said.

Rhandh pointed at the sea. "The Klar homeland lies there."

"Beneath the water?" I asked incredulously.

"Yes. The true base of the slavers lies beneath the island and beneath the sea. It is named Andertalen. The isle is called Talen. There is an opening from the island into the underground through one of the ancient lava funnels that poured out the magma to build the original volcano. The outflow of the lava left a vast cavern, dozens of verlangs in extent, below the surface."

"And that land is not flooded?" Heril asked.

"Part of it is, yes, but the land is shaped like a shallow bowl. The center is a broad lake but the rims of the bowl are dry land, kept that way by the pressure of the air trapped inside. The capital city of the Klar lies within, where their ruling council is seated and the records are kept. One task of their slaves is to reclaim more of the land."

I glanced at Jask. He was bound so that he could not leap overboard and swim to shore to warn his people. He only shrugged, but a slight smile twisted his lips.

"And what other purposes do the slaves serve?" Jedik asked.

"They grow food, for the Klar and for themselves," the Vlih said. "They dig in the mines and take from them rubies and great emeralds that their Klar masters work into jewelry for their own ears, and circlets for their arms and their females. The slaves dig and labor for the glory of the Klar. And they die."

He turned to me. "You were their slave but you were not intended for the mines. So they fed you well and did not flay the flesh from your bones with whips. They are not so kind to those they invite home with them."

He glanced then at Jask, and I could see that his hatred was very strong. Too, fear hid in his eyes, fear at what he had seen in Andertalen and at what he had suffered. Clearly, he did not wish to suffer it again. Yet, he mastered both his hate and his fear. He was an honorable and courageous man, and I call him "man" even though his race was Vlih. A man is something more than a heap of flesh and blood and bone piled into a specific container. Valyan's people have a saying, that the body does not matter, only the Khi. I have often heard similar sentiments expressed on Earth and I believe them to be true.

For a time, silence lingered among us as we digested Rhandh's words. Teware broke the quiet by asking something that lightened our mood.

"If this Andertalen lies under ground, then how do the people see?"

It was an issue none of us had thought of and most of us laughed that we hadn't. Even Rhandh smiled, the first time I had seen such an expression on his face. It made him look younger, as he must have looked before his pride had been broken.

"A wise question," Rhandh said to Teware. "But I will tell you what I have seen. There is a mineral in the cavern stone that gives off a blue glow. It is not like sunlight but is as bright as the outer world on a cloudy day and plants will grow beneath it.

"The oddest thing is that the glow dims and brightens in a regular cycle. For some ten dhaur (about thirteen hours) the light is bright enough to see by. Then it gradually wanes until night falls. It is a night such as you have never imagined, a night of absolute blackness. Only those who carry their light with them can move about at such a time."

"It must be the work of the Asadhie," Jedik said.

"Aye," agreed Rhandh, "or of the Thye Vessoth."

"I've heard of the Asadhie," Teware said, "but what are these Thye Vessoth?"

To my surprise, it was Jask who answered: "In legend they were once servants and priests of the snake god, Vessoth, and of his wife Vohanna, both of whom may have been Asadhie. Years ago their cult flourished among my people. But they were lovers of blood sacrifice, and they were overthrown. We Klar may be harsh but even we can have our fill of gore. The Thye Vessoth are evil incarnate and no one should have traffic with them who values his Khi."

Shuddering, I remembered the strange being that Bryce and I had seen on Earth, the being that Jedik had named a Thye Vessoth. Again I felt the crawling horror that had gnawed at my brain when I glanced into that creature's stone-blue eyes and heard its eerie words. Then the wind blew the Darkling out past the headland of the Klar isle and a cold rain, falling from great heights, wafted across us to obscure the lights of the land.

I turned to Rhandh. "You said there was a gate into Andertalen? Where is it and how heavily is it guarded?"

"Beyond the harbor lies an upper city," the Vlih said. "In its center is a temple dedicated to Heshval, the main Klar deity. The opening lies at the rear of the temple, behind the altar. It is closed with great bronze doors at night and mail-clad warriors stand constantly at the portal."

"How did you pass the gate when you escaped?" I asked him.

"I didn't."

"Then there is another entrance?" I asked.

"An exit, perhaps, but I think no one could enter there. Andertalen has many hot springs that provide fresh water to the Klar. Most give rise to streams that flow into the central sea, but there is one that runs only a few feet from where it wells up before diving into the earth through a lava vent. My escape came suddenly. I had not planned well and ended up cornered near that spring. I had no weapons with which to fight but could not let the Klar capture me again. I took my chance in the underground river.

"Luckily, the river came out in the ocean instead of pouring into the bowels of the planet. That river is a wild, racketing ride through the stone. There is no way of fighting it and no place where a pocket of air remains. I was near dead from lack of breath when the river vomited me out through a waterfall in the island cliff. Even if one could get up the sheer cliff forty feet to that opening, no one could swim that distance against the torrent."

I smiled. "Then we must pass through the main gate at the temple."

Rhandh looked at me and announced, rather dryly: "I fail to see the humor. But then perhaps you would also find amusement in walking into a Quaal's lair."

The Quaal is a predator, one of the most successful on Talera, and it will eat a man. It looks reptilian but is warm blooded and incredibly swift. The largest may weigh two tons. Like some species of Earth shark, the Quaal's needle teeth slant backward into its maw. What enters those alligator-shaped jaws makes no exit. However, I had no intention of "walking into a Quaal's lair."

"You will never reach the gates," Rhandh said.

I smiled again at him. "Perhaps not as ourselves," I agreed, "but as Klar...." Deliberately, I left the sentence unfinished.

The Vlih warrior spluttered. "Are you mad? We cannot pass as Klar."

I glanced at Heril and Valyan. They nodded and disappeared below deck.

"I am not mad," I said to Rhandh. "But wait for a moment and then decide for yourself."

We waited in the night with only a few shielded lanterns to cast a little light. The sound of surf boomed from everywhere. Heril and Valyan quickly returned with their arms full of sacks and bundles of clothing. Rhandh looked at me, arching one eyebrow.

"Close your eyes," I told him.

He shook his head, rather sadly I thought, but did as I asked. Humoring the insane, perhaps. I selected several bundles, removed their contents and donned them. I rubbed oil on my arms and chest and returned to stand before the Vlih.

"Well, what is going on?" he demanded.

"Do not open your eyes yet," I told him. "Do me one favor first."

"By the ice god's shades, what is it?"

"Smell," I told him. "Deeply."

He sniffed the salt air, then again. His nose wrinkled.

"What do you scent?" I asked him.

"Klar," he replied, and opened his eyes.

CHAPTER FIFTEEN

TEMPLE OF DARKNESS

We came from the barren north of the isle, drifting silently beneath a sky full of rain, and entered the Klar stronghold on Talen. The rain obscured the moons and left the night very dark. Lamps burned here and there, protected from the drizzle by metal shields that let little light fall on the streets. The city lay blunt and huge in the shadows, the buildings squatting low to the earth, laid out in rectangles and squares. It was an orderly arrangement but contained nothing of grace or beauty.

The Klar call their settlement Kwellarn. We entered it unopposed. The city had no walls and there seemed no guards, but then the Klar have few enemies powerful enough to attack them. Predators seldom stalk predators.

We had concocted a wild scheme, a bold stroke as subtle as a blow to the head. Portions of the plan had been laid while we were still in Emira. Because of their unique handicaps, and perhaps because of their technology, the Emirians were skilled artisans with masks and clothing. I had seen statues in Emira that I would have begged pardon of had I bumped into them on the streets. I had even seen miniatures that danced and sang like tiny people. For them to make a Klar was nothing.

Clay molds prepared from the heads and faces of the Klar that we had captured on Emira had been cast into exquisite masks of light metal. The craftsmen had, as well, fashioned body molds of cloth and wire, padded to give the impression of larger size and ingeniously constructed so that

114

they could be moved as easily as we moved our own limbs. Over these we had strapped the leathers taken from the captives, and Klar shields hung over our shoulders. The disguises were good and in the darkness and rain, seen only as silhouettes against flickering torches, we felt that we could pass for a bit.

We should be aided by the fact that the Klar depend more on their excellent sense of smell than do Humans, especially at night when their good diurnal vision is much reduced. Just as Humans wear silks and jewels for the aesthetic pleasure it brings, the Klar wear scents and oils and elaborate perfumes. We had confiscated a number of such ointments and had doused ourselves liberally with them. We now stank like Klar, though I suppose we might prove attractive to another of the beasts under the appropriate circumstances.

The second part of our plan was less well conceived. We knew from Rhandh that the gates to the underworld were well guarded but that the guards were switched at the twentieth dhaur, the equivalent of Earth's midnight. We would have to kill the replacements soon after the exchange. This should give us several dhaur in which to enter Andertalen and secret ourselves before the bodies were found.

Rhandh told us that the rim of the underworld cavern was thick with fallen blocks of stone, as well as being honeycombed with old lava vents. He assured us that a small army could hide there. Once under that cover we hoped to avoid detection long enough to reach the labor camps where the slaves toiled.

From there? Well, we would first have to locate our Koro friends, and Bryce and Eric if they could be found. We might then try to get them out through the exit Rhandh had used for *his* escape, or perhaps some other approach would suggest itself.

I also gave thought to Rannon and determined not to leave the pirate's homeland without her. She would be more difficult to locate because she was probably in the Klar capital rather than in the slave camps. But I would find her nevertheless. The Darkling would wait for us, or if need be would return.

Perhaps my hope of finding Rannon was a vain one.

Perhaps our entire plan was a fool's illusion. One does not simply walk into a slaver's hold and walk out with one's friends. I will only say in our defense that at the time it did not seem so difficult, caught up as we were in our feelings of shared danger.

Also, let me say that we had little choice. Andertalen had only one entrance that we knew of, the bronze gates in Kwellarn. Our friends, perhaps even members of our families, waited behind those gates. We could not leave them there. So, we pushed forward with our plan boldly, hoping that our daring would carry us through. We straightened our backs within our disguises and strode forward as conquerors, for, after all, were we not Klar?

Twelve disguises had been constructed but there were thirteen in our party. One of us did not need a mask. Just before the boat was lowered over the side of the Darkling to take us to shore I'd had Jask brought on deck.

I had then told the pirate: "You will take us along the most hidden ways to the temple of Heshval. It is necessary that we enter Andertalen."

"Of course not," he replied, smirking.

I sighed. "I will tell you, Jask. I would not wish to kill you, but my brother may be in there and I know that many of my friends are. I cannot allow your life to stand in the way of their freedom."

I drew my sword and placed it at his throat. "Now! I will say again. You will take us to the temple of Heshval."

Jask's umber eyes studied me. I do not think he believed that I would kill him. I did not believe it myself. But after a moment he blinked and murmured:

"Of course. You had only to ask."

Why had the former Klar commander not called my bluff? I did not know. But he led us now, with Rhandh and Heril at his sides to guard him. He did not try to escape.

For all our preparations, the city was silent, the streets empty and dark. It made me nervous that we met no Klar. Even Jask seemed at a loss to explain it.

The temple of Heshval lay nearly a verlang from where we had landed. We reached its steps almost at midnight. No torches gleamed in the bronze sconces that decorated the

116

walls; the doors stood open. We had come here unchallenged, our unease growing at each step of the way. The city was too empty, too silent. But we were committed now.

We waited for nearly five dhorrin (twenty minutes) outside the temple but when no guards came we slipped like ghosts up the long marble steps of the building and entered it. We found a cavernous place, without light save near the far end where a single fire burned in the pit of an obsidian altar. Stone pews were ranked and silent to either side of us in expectation of worshippers. The place smelled of smoke and of strange perfumes.

Beyond the altar and the fire that burned there, we saw the massive bronze doors that led into the underworld, into the true home of the Klar. They were closed and unguarded. The flames leaped and danced across them. Only one symbol marred the perfect reflecting surface of those gates, a stylized skull.

Such skulls show up again and again in the writing, and art, and religion of the Klar. They are a warrior race, a race who worship their ancestors and the glory of past deeds. They have many ceremonies that honor death in battle. Heshval the Conqueror is their god, and Rath, the Moon of Battle, and Klinsha, he who absorbs the spirits of the slain. As you might expect, lineages play an important role in their culture. He who has no ancestral line to call his own can have little power among them. Thus it was with Jask, the illegitimate son of a Klar noble.

Naturally, I was not thinking these thoughts at the time. I thought only of where the guards might be as we stalked forward down the aisle toward the waiting gates. Our footfalls echoed but brought no challenge.

"I do not like it," Rhandh said, "The way to Andertalen is never left unguarded."

"Except...." Jask began. But he did not finish.

The gates started to open. I did not see the massive counterweights and pulleys that must have been necessary to move all those tons of bronze. Nor did I hear them. In eerie silence the great doors opened outward, like some monstrous raptor spreading its wings. We stood in awe of that silence, unable for a moment to even breathe.

117

Then the hair crawled to life on my neck. Something black, of awesome size, moved amidst the darkness behind the gates. Shadows billowed. The shape came forward, as black as a night on which all the moons had fallen. For a moment, the wild thought struck me that the god Heshval had sensed our violation of its temple and had come to exact retribution.

The shape of the god came out into the temple, backlit by flickering torches. The eyes smoldered fifteen feet above the floor, flaming like bane fires. The body of the god was Klar, savagely scarred. The face was Klar as well, but twisted, as if with hate or lust.

I sensed the men around me drawing back. Only Jedik stood his ground with me. He drew his sword. It rasped against the sheath. We heard then the creak of ropes and the cadence of feet stamping against the stone floor. Green light burst suddenly upward, throwing the temple into emerald relief.

And we saw that the god was only a statue sculpted from black stone. Fifty Klar labored at its feet, each nearly seven feet in height. They leaned forward into leather harnesses, muscles bulging beneath their sweat-sheened hides as they pulled their god up the road from the underworld, almost as if they came from hell.

The statue rested on a wheeled platform and at its feet stood a figure with a fiery emerald wand in one hand. It was reptilian, like the Klar, but there the resemblance ended. It seemed a twin of the Thye Vessoth that I had once seen on Earth.

"Priests of evil," Jask had called them. "Lizards," Rhandh had said. "They had been overthrown," Jask had said.

It did not seem that way to me. Yet, when I stole a quick glance at our guide he seemed as surprised as I to find a Thye Vessoth in the temple of Heshval.

The lizard priest wore a scarlet robe sashed with yellow. A black dagger glittered in its right fist. The green wand was clutched in its left. At its feet lay another being, a Human. I glimpsed dark hair, white skin, and gleaming silver chains. I stepped forward and the priest saw us. I do not think our disguises fooled him.

The light blazed higher. The shadows that warded us were dispersed. The Thye Vessoth raised his knife and pointed at us. A word shrieked, like an iron claw torn across stone. I did not understand it.

The statue of Heshval ceased its forward movement, blocking the gate to Andertalen. I could hear a murmur from packed masses of Klar who stood behind the god. They could not see what occurred. But the beasts that pulled the statue saw. They raised their heads and shrugged out of their harnesses. Backs bent with exertion began to straighten. Axes flashed as they were drawn over shoulders. The Klar are never unarmed, even in their temples.

"We've got to get out of here," Rhandh stated flatly. "We've got to get out of here now!"

I heard the others step away from me but did not move. The Human chained at the feet of the obsidian god raised its head. Lustrous raven hair fell away from a pale, oval face and I saw the exquisite beauty of a woman. Those around me took another step backward. I took a step forward, then began to run madly toward the statue and the chained girl.

CHAPTER SIXTEEN

THE FIGHT BEFORE THE GATE

Through the aisle of the temple I ran, toward the dark god of the Klar and the woman chained at its feet. Jedik shouted behind me. I did not catch his words. Nor would it have mattered. The blood rushed in my veins; the wind of my passage tore at my hair. A sudden exultation swept through me. My sword slid free of its leather trappings and winked in the green light.

Then I was among the slavers who stood milling confusedly at the feet of their deity. I tore the mask from my face and hurled it into the snarling features of a Klar warrior. It struck him and he staggered backward. I ripped away the false breastplate covering my chest and let it drop. The beasts near me appeared startled. I killed one, driving my sword through its throat. The blade licked back and sideways. Blood spurted; a Klar screamed. An odor of fear and rage exploded into my nostrils like a heady perfume.

I cut my way toward the platform upon which the girl lay bound. And of a sudden there were allies with me, Jedik, and Heril Rolvfshern, and others. My friends. Rhandh picked up a massive Klar and hurled him into a row of enemies. Valyan's sword cleaved a slaver's chest. Heril's axe took off a face.

The Thye Vessoth priest saw what was happening. It grabbed the Human female by the hair and dragged her to her feet. Chains rattled. The priest raised its dagger, preparing to sacrifice its captive. Up the dirk went, its black curves absorbing the light. The girl must have been intended as an

120

offering to the god. Now the priest intended to finish the ritual.

"No!" I shouted.

The girl looked up at the creature. It stood taller than she by a head, its face suffused with rage, death glittering in its hand. But she did not flinch and a snarl of defiance twisted her beautiful lips. My thoughts applauded her.

Then the rapier was reversed in my fist and I threw it overhand like a knife. It went end over end and flew true. The blade entered beneath the Thye Vessoth's left arm. The being squalled like a stuck swine and dropped the dagger. The girl got a slim foot behind its leg and tripped it. It fell backward off the platform, dragging guards down with it. The crystal wand slipped from its clutches and rolled against the feet of the statue, continuing to flash out green bursts of light that threw into relief the area around it.

I ran forward, toward the dais. An axe crashed down at me. I caught it and held it, then smashed the Klar aside and took the weapon from its grip. The haft was sanded smooth, the wood warm from the touch of enemy hands. The broad, heavy blade lashed out, crushing mail into a slaver's chest and tearing away an arm. The Klar war axe is a frightful weapon.

I leaped onto the platform. The girl stood very still, wearing only her argent shackles and her pride. Her eyes met mine, clear and startling blue. She raised one dark eyebrow in question.

"My lady," I said, and with the axe I chopped through the chain that bound her to one massive leg of Heshval.

Around us, guards clambered onto the platform but Jedik and the others had reached us and they beat the slavers back. Steel whistled and rang all about us. Klar fell. Beings shrieked in pain and grunted with effort and strain. I ignored it all. The girl's eyes looked into mine. Those perfect lips opened. Her voice thrummed, deep and throaty and melodic.

"My thanks, Ruenn Maclang," she said.

"I did not realize I would find you again so soon, Rannon," I said. "Else I would have brought flowers."

She laughed. There in the midst of red battle, she threw back her head and laughed. She was then even more beautiful.

Suddenly, Rhandh appeared beside us, ripping through struggling bodies to fall on his knees before Rannon.

"Jhesana!" he cried.

The girl's gaze flickered from me to the kneeling warrior.

"Forgive me, Jhesana," Rhandh said. "Twice I failed you. Once when I could not prevent your abduction, and again when I thought you dead and did not search."

This puzzled me.[3] But I did not say that there was no time for it. For a moment we held our own against superior odds. The battle surged around us but did not sweep us away. A Klar rushed upon me. I killed him and let his life spill on the wood of the dais. With the axe handle I blocked a short sword thrust at my heart. My fist smashed a guard's nose into ruins.

Yet, part of my mind heard Rannon's reply to the dark warrior. She stood there in a frothing mist of savagery and death and took a moment to restore to a wounded man his pride. She put a hand on his shoulder. The manacles that still clasped her wrists jingled with her movements.

"You have not failed me, Rhandh. For you are here now."

Hearing her words, I knew without a doubt that I loved her. I glanced once at Rhandh, saw his shoulders straighten. His eyes blazed as he shoved the black mane of hair from his face. He rose, sword glittering in his fist. His tail whipped

---

[3] I learned later that Rannon had been abducted by Durhain, who apparently wanted her for himself. Durhain was a noble in her homeland and was apparently selling his own people out to the Thye Vessoth and the Klar.

There had, it seemed, been an earlier attempt to kidnap Rannon, also engineered by Durhain, which failed. During the course of that attempt, Rhandh—whose Vlih NHa made up Rannon's bodyguards—had been captured and taken to Andertalen. The other members of the band had been killed. Rhandh thought Rannon was taken in that raid and that she must have been killed because he heard nothing of her in the Klar hold. It was this incident he referred to when he said that he had twice failed her. In reality, she had been almost miraculously saved during the first kidnapping attempt.—Ruenn Maclang.

about his legs.

"Hold them!" I shouted to Jedik and the others as they faced the tide of our enemies. And they held them.

I turned and grabbed Rhandh before he could leap into the fray. "Rannon!" I shouted at him. "Your Jhesana. She must be saved. We will anchor them here until you escape."

He struggled for a moment and then my words registered and he nodded.

"No!" Rannon said. "I will not allow you to sacrifice yourselves for me."

"We do not," I said. "We will follow after you've gotten out of the temple. But we must disengage slowly or we'll all be cut down."

Still, I saw defiance in her face. She did not wish to leave us to die. So I said something cruel. "We have no time to free you of your chains now, my lady. You will only slow us and none of us will escape."

Her eyes flashed but her gaze did not waver. Then she nodded. She made her decisions quickly, did this girl, and she believed what I said about following them even though I knew that I lied. The slavers were still slowed by the surprise of our onslaught and by the death of the priest. That could not last. Those Klar who were trapped behind the statue would be upon us in a moment. Even now I felt the platform beneath me move as they shoved it forward out of the way. Yes, I had lied to Rannon. We could never disengage from so many.

But the girl believed me. "Very well," she said.

Rhandh took her up in one arm and leaped from the dais. His brand gleamed freshly red before he reached the door. The rest of us retreated slowly, guarding the escape of the Vlih and of Rannon. We had lost two men, both of them ex-slaves, but we had chosen only the best fighters from among our crew and many more than two of the enemy had died.

I could see no sign of Jask and wondered briefly why he was not with the other Klar. I did not think of it for long. Another of our men dropped and we drew together in a semicircle, keeping the Klar in front of us. Steadily backward, we worked our bloody way, though most of the gore that covered us was not our own. Our foes did not seem overly eager to engage. Many bled from bitter wounds and their priest lay in a torn wreck at the feet of their god.

And still we withdrew. Rhandh and the girl had made it through the door. We, too, neared it, and for a moment I thought—I hoped—that we might be able to disengage before enemy reinforcements arrived.

That hope shattered as a roar went up. A glance told me that the statue had cleared the gates. Shadowy figures poured quickly out from behind it. Many carried torches, which splashed fresh light on the scene to replace the waning emerald glow of the Thye Vessoth's wand. The newcomers surged forward and we were thrown back, no longer retreating at our will but pushed by the superior weight of our attackers.

The fight turned savage. Steel clashed and shrilled more loudly. Spittle flew as men and Klar fought and clawed and cursed each other from a distance of inches. Jedik raged like a demon, his sword a living brand of steel that sent foe after foe to hell.

We stabbed and parried, shouted and beat and groaned. And Klar died. But they could replace their dead and we could not. One of Jedik's men collapsed beside me. I had no chance to see who or what had killed him as I slid a blow from an axe that would have crushed my ribs. The hook on the reverse of my own axe tore out the beast's throat. Its scream was born and stillborn in red froth.

Jedik glanced at me. His teeth flashed in a brief smile. "There may be hope for your skills yet!" he shouted, sliding his sword into his own opponent with an economy of movement that I envied. He struck well, but not deeply. In a battle like this, a sword left too long in the body of a foe meant you were dead.

A Koro fell, his head smashing backward from his shoulders, his neck spurting blood from where a Klar axe had been buried into his lower face and throat. I killed that beast, but there were plenty to replace him. The slavers grew more and more frenzied as the battle continued, as the scent of pain and rage filled their sensitive nostrils. They launched themselves upon us with power and ferocity, hacking in an orgy of hatred. And we matched them.

124

But there were too many of them for us to win. At last they broke our defense apart. Isolated, we were cut down. I saw Heril driven to his knees, saw him stagger up again, his axe flashing and bloody. I cut a swath toward him, Jedik at my back. Valyan was gone; I knew not where.

We reached Heril and the three of us stood with our backs to the temple wall. Our weapons leaped and gleamed, spattering crimson drops. Heril fought on my right, Jedik on my left. The Emirian was a master, weaving a maze of brilliant steel around us in the torchlight. Each of us would have been dead a dozen times if it had not been for his skill.

Yes, Jedik's sword flamed. Then it ceased flaming. There came a grunt and he stumbled hard against me. I dropped the axe and caught up Jedik's rapier in my right hand, the Emirian himself in my left. The sword leaped out as if on its own and parried a thrust from a Klar brand. The axe clattered on the cold hardness of the floor. And a dark arrow stood out of Jedik's chest. I did not see the archer but knew him to be skilled to hit his target in such a crowd.

Jedik looked at me. His eyes flashed once. "It was...," he said, and was gone.

At that moment a red-hot pain smashed my left shoulder. I was hurled backward against the wall with the shock of the arrow, crying out as I involuntarily dropped Jedik. I got the sword up to deflect a second arrow but could not block a blade that razored into my side. I killed the one who had struck me and caught a second sword on mine and drove it to the floor.

The hook of an axe chopped into my calf and I went to one knee, then got my feet under me again and stood. I parried a killing thrust and ducked beneath a flashing black arrow that caromed off the wall. The archer had to be in a balcony to look down on me in the swirling melee of the battle.

I took the hand off of an attacker. I could no longer see Heril. I shouted for him but heard nothing in response. The flat of an axe glanced off my shoulder. My legs gave from under me and I fell. My body was too numb for pain but there was much blood, and now a lot of it was mine. I fell forever it seemed, a wild buzzing in my ears. Then my head struck stone and darkness welled up.

Swords of Talera, by Charles Allen Gramlich

I am dead, I thought, and knew no more.

CHAPTER SEVENTEEN

CONDEMNED

I did not die, but that was not necessarily a blessing. I awoke to pain, to hot and brutal agony that cycled in time with my breathing. My body felt clammy and constricted and I realized after a moment that I was swathed in bandages that were wet with sweat.

I opened my eyes. That was not as easy as it sounds for they were gummed tightly shut. I was lying on a cot in a long, low, narrow room built of reddish stone. Dim bluish light filtered through a dozen small, barred windows high on the walls. Unless the sun had changed colors again, which of course was possible, I was not under the skies of Talera.

Someone cleared their throat in the room. It was Heril, seated on a nearby cot. His left arm and shoulder were bandaged, but he was smiling.

"The joke escapes me," I croaked.

His grin widened. "We came to rescue the slaves and we end up here," he said, waving his good hand at our prison. "Is this not humorous?"

I had to admit that it was. "But where is here?" I asked.

"In Andertalen. In an empty slave barracks, I think."

"How long?"

"A day, day and a half. How do you feel?"

"Excellent," I replied. "And you?"

"A broken arm, no more."

"Have you heard anything of Rhandh and the girl?" I asked.

"Nothing."

"Let's hope that's a good sign."

"Yes."

"What of Valyan?"

"He lives," Heril said, "but is badly hurt. Our captors came and got him a little while ago for some type of *treatment*. They said he would be returned."

"Anyone else?"

"No one of ours," the blond Koro said. "Nor have I seen Jask. I assume he's free among his people now."

"And Jedik is dead," I murmured.

"Aye," Heril replied. He was no longer smiling and there was pain in his eyes.

To break a growing silence, I said: "I wonder why we are still alive?"

"I think they want to hurt us," Heril replied.

Again there was quiet. I started to say something inane but the door opened and a Klar entered. Others of his kind followed but I watched only the first. In his hands, I knew, our fate rested.

The beast was tall and spare, with skin the color of old mahogany. His features were harsh and predatory, savage and arrogant; his eyes shone a dark gold around large pupils. He wore little in the way of clothing, only a short black and yellow kilt of snakeskin. This he had belted with a red sash from which protruded a short sword similar to the wakizashi of the samurai. Silver earrings glittered at his lobes, shaped like crooked daggers, and a ring was on his left index finger. It held a red stone carved in the likeness of a skull, with gold buttons for eyes. He strode over to the foot of my bed. His eyes blazed upon us. I could smell him, like cinnamon and sand. Even his scent seemed angry, though not unpleasant.

"Where is the Vlih dog that was with you in the temple?" he demanded in thickly accented Koro. "And where did he take the female slave?"

My heart leaped. So, Rannon had not been recaptured. She and Rhandh must have reached the ship and be well away by now.

"Answer me," the Klar commanded.

"I don't think I want to tell you," I said to him.

Heril winced.

The Klar's golden eyes narrowed. "You have much arrogance, Human," he said. "It will kill you some day. Perhaps soon."

I did not reply.

"Why were you in the temple?" he asked.

"We could not allow the sacrifice of the girl," I said.

"Instead, you sacrifice yourselves?"

I did not shrug for fear the pain would make me wince. I did not wish to show weakness before this being. He would fasten upon it and use it against us.

"That was not our intention either," I told him.

"You have blasphemed our god," he continued. "For that, the penalty can be no less than death."

"Then why have you left us alive?" I asked him.

"We wished you to know that you would die, and the manner of it."

I did not speak.

"You have heard of the lava mines of Andertalen?"

"No," I said.

He smiled, mirthlessly. "Then I will tell you of them.

"In those pits lurid flames light constantly the pressing stone. There is little oxygen and the very air burns with heat. One quickly becomes dehydrated. Water is plentiful on the walls but it is not fit to drink. It boils hot to the touch and stinks with mineral poisons. Yet, men drink it and scream in agony as it rips at them.

"Steam rises constantly there, obscuring the vision and tearing the lungs from a man as the work tears the flesh from his bones. Slaves do not live long in the mines but many of them say it is too long. They beg for mercy and it is not given. They beg for release and it is withheld. When they finally collapse, and they all do, their bodies are left to rot in the foul air of the deeper caverns where even larts will not venture, though food be plentiful. Their deaths mean nothing. The work goes on night and day. Slaves die and are replaced and are quickly forgotten by their fellows. Such are the mines of the Klar."

It sounded like hell to me.

"I take it we are to have the honor of serving there," I said.

"Yes," the beast agreed, "but not until you have healed. We wish you to be healthy when you are taken to the mines. Thus, your agony will be prolonged."

"You are too kind," I said dryly.

"I am," he said. "But I cannot think of a just punishment for what you have done."

I believe he meant it.

Oddly enough, I did not hate him. In his eyes we had blasphemed his god. Well, we had. Would men of Earth behave differently under similar circumstances? I think not and I call to mind many on our world who have died for their beliefs, or lack of them, at the hands of those who considered themselves holy men.

"One thing more," the Klar said.

"What?" I asked.

"I would have the names of those I condemn to death."

"I am Heril," said Heril the Koro.

"And I am Ruenn Maclang," I told him.

"I will give you my name also," the Klar said, "so that you may have someone to curse while you are in mines. I am called Relic, high priest of Heshval."

"Servant of the Thye Vessoth," I added.

That stung him. His eyes narrowed.

"Speak not of what you know not, Human. The Thye Vessoth have come to aid us. They, too, serve the will of Heshval."

"Of course," I said.

He looked at me for a space longer. "I know of the Koro," he said, "but I have never heard such a name as yours. What does it mean?"

"It means that I will be back for you," I said.

A lean warrior beside Relic—with light, almost green skin—leaped forward, hauling at his rapier. I think he would have killed me but the high priest held up a hand, in his eyes a grudging respect.

"You have courage, Human," he said. "It is a pity that the mines will break you of it."

There was no answer to that.

He turned away. The door closed behind them all and Heril and I were left alone.

The Koro chortled. "I think you are insane, Ruenn, but at least you're not boring."

I laughed a little with him but it hurt so badly that I quit.

* * * * * * *

Time passed swiftly as we healed. The Klar put us under the care of female slaves adept at changing our bandages and easing our pain. They could not sooth our worries. Valyan was not returned to us and the guards would tell us nothing though I raged and cursed at them. We feared that he was dead and I vowed to myself that this was one more debt that must be paid. But our plans for escape and vengeance were only plans for we had no chance to implement any of them. Our jailers stood always near.

The three slaves assigned to care for us were Kaldi, a populous race found scattered widely across Talera. The females are near the size of Human women while the males are generally larger and heavier than men. Both sexes are covered with short fur, commonly of a reddish color. The female's fur is silken to the touch, the male's shorter and more coarse. Their features are Human-like and quite pleasing.

It is said that the Kaldi make good slaves, but I have seen their warriors—and their women too—fight and know them to be a courageous people. They are a practical race and accept what they feel they cannot change, and it is probably for this reason that they are called good slaves. I think there are no races that make good slaves. All die without freedom.

When I was able to get up after a few days we were allowed, with guards, to venture out into Andertalen. I know what I had expected from Rhandh's brief description of the underworld but this was no collapsed caldera of an extinct volcano. It was far too vast. The ceiling hung half a verlang (three quarters of a mile) over our heads, partially hidden by a gauzy mist through which massive stalactites surged like fangs. Surely this was not a naturally formed cavern. I remembered Jedik speculating that it might have been made by the Asadhie. Well, if they could create all of Talera then dry land beneath the ocean should pose little problem for them.

131

Andertalen even had a wind, or rather a breeze that stirred off the cool water of the central sea. It stank slightly of chemicals but that scent was largely overridden by a salt tang. As Rhandh had said, the place was shaped like a bowl with the central portion of the bowl filled with the sea. The shore lay a good distance from where we stood. The water was the familiar dark blue, darker than the light it reflected.

The light was not produced by any sun but by chemical reactions in the stone of the cavern. It spilled from the roof, and elsewhere from cyclopean blocks of fallen granite and outcroppings of bare rock that thrust up through the thin soil. We could see clearly by the light but could not see far because of a haze that shrank distance.

The haze cut off vision to the north and east. The southern wall was at our backs, half a verlang away. We could also see the western wall, or sections of it that weren't hidden by the buildings of a city whose spires rose stolid and massive. This was Kwellarn, or rather the part of the city that lay beneath the island. It was called Kwellarn the Lower. Like an iceberg, the portion below was much larger than the portion above.

Kwellarn appeared to be the only large population center but a number of red-stone buildings clustered around the central sea. That sea was large enough so that I could not see across it, and oar-driven ships plied its surface. Crops grew near the shore and herds of terval, the short-horned cattle of Talera, and of the ox-like stugah grazed on the mossy, blue-stemmed grass that carpeted the floor of the cavern.

I did not see many Klar, though the Kaldi who tended us said that the total population of the pirate's hold was about seventy thousand. This did not count slaves, who probably numbered another fifteen thousand or so. I saw more of the slaves than of their masters. They labored in the fields and watched over the herds. Most were either Human or Kaldi, but I glimpsed a few others.

A Green Llurn came past us one day driving a small herd of terval, and I almost mistook him for Valyan. As he came closer, though, I noticed that he had only one eye and that his right leg had been broken long ago and set poorly. I saw, also, several Llurns with black skin and silver hair and eyes. Their arrogance showed even beneath their chains. I watched them watching the Klar and did not think they took well to slavery.

I have just mentioned two of the Llurn races of Talera, the emerald and the ebon, the former of which call themselves Nakscherii. There are more. Among them are the golden Llurns, who are like beautiful statues made of incarnate gold, and the indigo Llurns, whose skin is purple or blue and whose eyes can be a dozen pastel colors. They are perhaps the most striking of all the Llurns. All of these races were once bred from Human stock. In most cases they can intermarry with true Humans and produce children, though such offspring are themselves usually sterile.

Eventually, of course, I saw representatives of most of the peoples of Talera among the slave population in Andertalen. The Klar are indiscriminate in their raiding.

Heril and I were also their captives—again—but they treated us well while we healed. They often let us walk down to the seashore and even to the outskirts of Kwellarn the Lower, where Klar and their slaves swarmed about a myriad daily tasks. We were fed twice a day on meat and fresh vegetables, and were occasionally given sweet wine. In the evenings, the slave girls played music and danced for us.

It seemed almost as if the Klar were determined to show us how pleasant life in Andertalen could be, perhaps so that we would have good memories to contrast with the horrors of the lava mines. That sojourn was soon to begin.

Chapter Eighteen

The Lava Mines

They came for us on a morning when rain fell on the roof of our prison. I awoke to the sound of it and went to the door to look out at a gray world of mist. Four guards stood at the entrance, impervious to the drizzle that beaded on their bullet heads and scaled bodies. They pointed crossbows at me when I opened the door. I smiled and held up my hands but their expressions did not change.

Heril joined me. "Dour looking bunch," he said, motioning at the guards.

"Aye," I replied. "And such sweet dispositions."

We laughed.

"Where do you think the rain comes from?" Heril asked.

"The central sea, I imagine. And the springs. The haze we've been seeing must be evaporation. But the water vapor can't escape through the cavern roof so it eventually condenses under its own weight and sprinkles down. I would guess it falls periodically. The temperature never seems to change much here so the evaporation and condensation rate must be fairly constant."

"It should be enough to keep things growing anyway," Heril said, without much real interest.

I heard something then and did not reply. It sounded like the creak of an ungreased wagon axle. A moment later the wagon that went with the sound materialized out of the mist, pulled by two of the ox-like stugah. Half a dozen guards squatted beneath a hide canvas that covered the rear of the conveyance.

Riding ahead to avoid the mire came a tall, lean Klar that I recognized. It was he whom Relic—the high priest—had kept from killing me on the day that we had been sentenced to the lava mines. This Klar's name was Truen. A strange design upon his shield, a spiral with a hawk in the center, indicated his clan affiliation. A dull grayish medallion around his throat was engraved with another symbol that showed his noble birth and the level at which he stood in the Klar hierarchy.

The mount that Truen rode is called a tasaber. It resembles a large member of the deer family but has long been domesticated. It is a breed known for courage, endurance, and strength. Tasabers are quite a bit larger than horses, averaging above twenty hands. Incidentally, there *are* horses on Talera. Their ancestors were brought from Earth. There are also a dozen other riding animals on the planet but I think none can match the horse or the tasaber. The latter is a spirited beast whose heart is always given fully when it is given.

The particular individual that Truen rode was a little shorter than average, around twenty hands. It had a burnt umber coat and long legs that looked fragile for its bulk. It lacked a mane, which meant it was female. The males have coarse manes and horns as well, though the latter are usually removed. Both sexes have long tails similar to a horse's.

Tasabers generally do not care for Klar, probably because of their smell, which is strong and musty. Truen's mount seemed accepting enough of its lot, though it frequently snorted through its nostrils and pranced and danced and had to be held with a tight rein. I saw Truen's hands on those reins and my lips thinned. His fists gripped tightly, hauling back on the silver bit, and I thought he held the beast in too cruelly.

Heril, too, saw the tasaber and the one who rode it, and he knew what they were here for. "Oh hell," he said. Of course, he did not use those exact words but that was what he meant. He actually said *"Sae Yaal shei,"* which means, "by Yaal's cavern"—Yaal being a god of hell in the pantheons of several Taleran races, including the Koro.

Yaal is only one of numerous gods and devils that Talerans can call on. Religion, like everything else here, is extremely complicated, as you might expect when the beliefs of a dozen or more worlds have been transplanted to the same fertile ground.

Truen dismounted in front of us, handing the tasaber's reins to one of the guards.

"Your recovery is at an end, Humans," he sneered, making the last word sound like a curse. "Now you will begin to pay for your blasphemy."

"Doesn't seem to trouble you much," I said.

"You are right," he replied. "I welcome it."

He waved a hand at his guards. "Bind them. Their destiny awaits."

I noticed the eyes of the guards as they watched the movements of their lean, arrogant commander, and I thought there was little love for Truen even among his own kind. Despite that, or perhaps because of it, they moved very quickly to carry out his orders. We were forced to strip and our hands were bound in front of us with leather straps. Long leashes ran from those straps to the back of the wagon, and the conveyance started with a jerk as the driver turned the stugah back around the way they had come.

So, shivering beneath the chilling rain, our feet and legs muddy, Heril and I began our journey to the lava mines—to our destiny, Truen had said. Apparently, we would have to walk to that destiny.

The wagon was rolling downhill at first and moved at a smart pace. But we kept up, plodding along in the ruts left by the iron-bound wheels. Mud thrown back from those wheels spotted us from head to toe. More mud clogged our feet and before long each step required a painful effort. But still we kept up.

Soon, the wagon started uphill, and though the stugah slowed we slowed even more. The distance turned behind us as a plough turns soil, but we seemed to get no closer to any destination. Truen rode beside us, chaffing at the pace held to by the stolid, placid stugah. I think he would have preferred that we be run to our fate.

I looked across at Heril. His lips whitened with pain as his newly healed arm jerked out in front of him with each lurch of our passage. He did not cry out. My own shoulder

136

grew numb where the arrow had struck it; my injured leg trembled with the strain and threatened to collapse under me. Neither of us would let ourselves fall, however. That would mean dragging, for I did not think Lord Truen would let the wagon stop long enough for us to rise.

On and on we went. At first I studied the increasingly rough land through which we passed, noting anew how large this underground cavern seemed. But soon my mind grew numb with the repetitive, monotonous movement of lifting one foot and then the other, one and then the other. My chin sank toward my chest. I lost track of time and distance; I lost track of thoughts. I did not even know we had stopped until my churning legs struck the rear of the wagon. I looked up and a booted foot caught me in the chest, sending me sprawling in the mud. I struggled to rise and felt Heril's bound hands beneath my arm, helping me. The rain had not stopped but had slowed to an even finer mist.

Guards piled out of the wagon. Our hands were unleashed and pulled behind us to be locked in irons. Heril winced with fresh pain as his injured arm was bent backward, but for me it was an almost welcome change of position. Truen came over as more chains were brought. I heard them rattle as they were locked around Heril's ankles.

The eyes of the Klar noble burned at me. Hatred filled them, not for what we had done in Heshval's temple but because we were Human and not Klar. He held a short, broadbladed whip in one hand and ached to use it. I did not want to start trouble, or perhaps I was learning. I looked away from his gaze.

"Look at me, Human, when I am standing before you," he demanded.

I looked at him and he spat in my face.

Well, maybe I wasn't learning. My feet had not yet been shackled. I took one of them and smashed it into the inside of Truen's left knee. Bone ground against bone. He screeched in pain and staggered back. His damaged leg gave out and he fell on his backside into the mire.

Hands grabbed for me. I ducked beneath them and the guard who'd made the grab stumbled past. I caught his leg with a foot, tripping him, and he went sliding on his face into the ooze. I kicked another Klar in the stomach and as he jackknifed I spun and caught him in the face with the heel of my other foot. He dropped like a clubbed ox.

A whip snaked out. The leather tangled around my legs and jerked them from under me. I fell heavily, face first in the muck. Guards leaped on me. I was dragged helplessly to my feet, spitting out mud and slime and a piece of someone's ear that I had bitten off in the pile.

Truen had been helped to stand, his face mottled green and white with rage. He had lost his whip but his mailed fist lashed out and crunched into my chin, snapping my head back. He kicked me in the groin and I doubled over, retching. He kicked me again, narrowly missing my face as I pulled it aside. Other blows rained down heavily. They added only increments to the bright glow of agony that already racked me.

Though beaten to my knees, I did not lose consciousness. I dimly recall being dragged through long corridors of rough stone and slammed up against a wall where manacles were locked on my wrists and ankles. I didn't know the Klar guards had left until Heril began calling me and I forced open my eyes.

Gradually, complete awareness returned. I straightened up a bit, taking some of the strain off my manacled arms. We had been hung against the slimy walls of a cavern. Chemicals in that slime stung savagely in my lacerations.

"You all right?" Heril asked after I finally managed to acknowledge his frantic calls for my attention.

"Possibly," I rasped in answer. "What did I miss?"

"Almost your own death," he said. "I think Truen would have killed you if the Captain of the Guard had not convinced him that the high priest would be most wroth. You've made an enemy, though."

"He was already my enemy," I said.

"Yes, I suppose he was."

I looked about. There was plenty of light to see by for the walls consisted of that stone which burns blue and makes the days of Andertalen. The light was not as bright here, however, as it had been closer to the surface.

"I assume they don't mean for us to starve to death

while we're hanging on these walls?" I said to Heril by way of a question.

"I don't think so," he replied. "The guard captain told me, rather gleefully, that someone would be along in a bit to collect us."

"Gleefully?" I asked.

"Well, he didn't make it sound as if we would enjoy the experience."

"I can hardly wait," I said.

Heril chuckled.

We joked on in that way for a time, until we could find no more to joke about. Gradually, we lapsed into silence. The cavern was not so quiet around us. We heard distant, echoing rumbles and rustling sighs, occasional titters. Over it all came the monotonous drip of water.

The louder sounds frightened us at first, chained as we were helplessly to the wall. At any moment we expected some horror to come slithering out of the deeper caverns to feed, but nothing disturbed us. Time passed, though it could not be measured, for the blue chemical light of the stone did not seem to cycle here as it did in Andertalen. Before long we ceased to respond even to sounds and drifted slowly into a torpor.

So, we were barely aware when at last a pattern developed in those sounds, a pattern of approaching footsteps punctuated by the grind of stone on stone. My head hung dully on my chest. I raised it only when the stench of torches cut through the fog in my brain. The wall across from me slid aside, leaving a wide doorway. A being stood in it. It was larger than a man, its bulk filling the opening in the wall.

"A Syber," Heril breathed.

The Syber's skin was gray and hairless. It had four arms and two legs, all massively muscled. A tail, tufted at the tip, twitched behind it. Its face resembled a bat's, with squat up-turned features, dark beady eyes, and ribbed ears. Needle sharp teeth flashed behind thin, red lips. A yellow whip coiled about its upper left arm. The hilt of a broadsword protruded over its right shoulder. Though completely naked, nothing indicated whether it was male or female.

Heril told me later that the Syber protect their genitalia by drawing them up inside their bodies, lowering them only when they are about to mate. This one was male as it turned out, but that makes no difference to a Syber. There is no sexual dimorphism among them and the only way to tell them apart is if their genitalia are extruded. They are one race where males and females are completely equal, if only in cruelty.

Behind the Syber stood a number of other beings. Each carried a whip and a stave, and some had copper-headed lances as well. Some were Human, others not, but they all resembled each other in the sadism on their faces.

Only the features of the Syber were unreadable. Its black eyes watched us. The whip slid down its arm and uncoiled in its hands. It spoke, seemingly in echoes, its voice grating and harsh. Only with difficulty could I understood its words, though the language was that of the Klar, with which I had become familiar.

"My name is Rathgar," it said. "I am now your master. There are but two rules here, work, and unquestioning obedience to my commands. There is only one punishment for transgression—death.

"These also are slaves," it said, motioning to the beings behind it, "but you will obey their commands as if they were mine. Do you understand?"

Neither Heril nor I spoke.

Rathgar shook out the whip and walked toward us. "I do not wish to repeat myself," it said.

I did not wish to feel the lash. "We hear you clearly," I said.

"That is well."

The Syber removed a key from a pouch at its side and unlocked our manacles. I rubbed my wrists where they had been chafed raw by the metal.

"Let us go," the creature said, motioning toward the doorway through which it and the others had come.

The guards moved around us and pushed us forward. We went with them, deeper into the tunnels that lie even beneath Andertalen. Soon, the walls stopped glowing as we dipped below the level of the blue chemical. I saw now what the torches were for, but I could not understand why these corridors had not filled with water for we must be a mile beneath the sea. I thought once again of the mysterious Asadhie, the beings who had created this world. Was this more of their work?

As we went down I began to notice an increase in heat, and the air around us seemed to grow lighter. Slowly, the torches were conquered by blooming orange and red shadows. The heat continued to intensify. Steam was soon rising from the wet walls until it seemed that we moved through a burning house. Our lungs labored to draw in enough of the stinking air.

Suddenly, we walked out of the cavern onto a ledge that extended over a vast, boiling sea of lava. I looked down and saw many beings toiling on great scaffolds and winding trails that seemed to rise out of the magma. It could have been a scene of the inferno.

"Welcome to the lava mines," one of our guards said.

CHAPTER NINETEEN

TO TOUCH THE DAGGER
AND BE NOT CUT

In the lava mines of Andertalen the heat and the labor stomps on a man and grinds him beneath its heel. It seizes on the soul, or the Khi as the Talerans call it, and stretches it thin, and breaks it if it can. Many men go insane in the mines. I have seen them run screaming to throw themselves into the lava baths, which make liquid out of stone. I have seen them dead in their cells of a morning, unable to face another day of agony.

But death is common in the mines. One quickly gets inured to it. It is those you find gibbering in a corner of their cells in the night, more animal than man, that you do not become accustomed to—that and the raw sound of falling whips and the odor of burnt flesh.

Beings grow weak and fail in the mines, or cunning and cruel and are rewarded with whips that they can use on their fellows. There are no free men in those burrows, only whip slaves and work slaves. But among the condemned there are always a few who grow neither weak nor cunning, but savage. You can see the cold in their eyes to match the heat around them. And it is in their walk that they seek always for a way to retake their freedom and repay their captors. Heril was one such, and I another. We talked when we could, softly.

There were eighteen others on our chain. Most had seen too much of the mines and any semblance of spirit had been beaten out of them. A few others still retained a bit of pride, a thin Kaldi whose shackles had worn away the fur at his wrists and ankles, an Ebon Llurn with only the stubble of his silver hair left, and one other Human, a broad, heavy man with a bald head and dull ferocity in his eyes. Vriun was the Kaldi, Devous the Llurn. The Human was called Kreeg.

These three we felt out about escape. Vriun listened. The Llurn disdained us. We were cautious around Kreeg. Clearly, he hated the overlords, but I did not completely trust him. And I did not believe him to be as dull as he acted. Vriun told us that he had once been a fighting slave of the Klar. His crime: strangling his master with his bare hands. I did not doubt that he had the strength for it, and it would take much strength for a Human to kill a Klar with only his hands.

At night we slept in our own sweat, in a tiny cell with the others of our chain. During the day the lava and the heat made our world. Of course, no real night or day existed in the burrows. Shifts of slaves labored at all hours. When our chain worked we called it day; when we did not we called it night. Our duties were not easy. The Klar used frozen lava to build their palaces and temples, and when the mines were first opened the slaves had spent their time cutting blocks of the stuff by hand.

During that cutting, some ten years before, workers had broken through a wall into a central vent where lava welled up continuously. Now, slaves labored—and we among them—at channeling the lava out of the central pit into cooler tunnels where it could be poured into large molds of metal. There, the lava set up into standard sized blocks that were then hauled away to be used for buildings to glorify the masters. Our masters.

This was not the only form of slavery in the mines. In due course, if one lived, one might graduate to some of the other corridors where the workers sifted through tons of ore to find a handful or two of rainbow jewels to decorate Klar nobles. The temperatures were not so extreme there. Deaths were fewer. I doubted that Heril and I would ever be assigned such lighter duties. The Klar would wish us to be worked until we collapsed. I determined not to collapse so that I might spite them.

One intriguing thing that I noted was that the metal

molds into which the lava was poured had to be periodically replaced. Heat will temper steel but it leaves metal that is left too long in its embrace brittle. I began taking every opportunity to let my leg chains dangle in the lava. It did not take long for them to grow white hot. I stood it as long as possible, until blisters rose, before letting them cool to be reheated again and again.

Although we were called a "chain," that was just a convenient designation for a work crew and we were seldom shackled together. Each night in our cell I was able to crawl away by myself and scrape at the superheated links. I used the loose stones of the floor, which were the only abrasives available, wrapping them in my rags to muffle the sound. And the iron links weakened.

Few of the others seemed to notice my actions. Most were too apathetic to do more at the end of a shift than swallow a few mouthfuls of gruel and collapse. I spoke to Heril and the Kaldi—Vriun—and they too worked stealthily at their chains. To cover up the white shine of the abraded metal we used the thick black grease that caked the bottom of our communal feeding trough. We were not discovered, and the links weakened.

The days ran together in the pits and Heril and I did not satisfy our captors by dying. We grew hard and strong with our labors, and our anger grew even stronger. Beings faded and failed and were taken away as corpses. New slaves came. The chain endured.

Several times we saw Koro that Heril knew. He acknowledged them with slight nods but we found no opportunity to speak with any of them. There was no word or sight of Bryce, nor any sign of my old ship's crew from Earth. I had not really expected to find them here, though seeing the Thye Vessoth in the temple had raised my hopes. The chances of discovering them in the hands of the Klar had been slight anyway. It was only that I'd known of no other place to look. Still, there were many slaves we had not seen. I would examine each of them if necessary.

I also kept my ears open for mention of Rhandh or Rannon. Although news trickled slowly down to the tunnels we did eventually hear most of what went on in the Klar world. This information came mainly from city slaves who had committed some transgression that earned them a sentence in the mines. There continued to be silence on the subject of my friends, though. I hoped that meant they were still free.

I did, however, learn something else of great interest. I had wondered at the presence of the Thye Vessoth in the city of the Klar. According to Jask, the one-time covenant between the two races had been broken long ago. After seeing the Vessoth priest in the temple, I'd assumed the pirate captain had lied. Actually, Jask had been telling the truth as far as he knew it. The new alliance between Klar and Thye Vessoth had come about only recently, in the months that Jask had been gone to sea, first as a slaver and later as a captive.

The lizard priests had apparently convinced the Klar religious hierarchy that their deity, Heshval, was somehow intertwined with the god Vessoth. The night we had come to the temple had been the night when the union between the two peoples was to be sealed with the sacrifice of Rannon. We had interrupted the ceremony and caused great confusion among the slavers and the Thye Vessoth. Many Klar had seen it as an ill omen for the coming union, and it had apparently taken some time to restore order. No wonder we were hated.

I confess that I was not terribly heartbroken to find that we had disrupted the Thye Vessoth's activities. The Klar are arrogant and often cruel, but they love their children and their families. They understand the concepts of courage and honor. The Thye Vessoth know none of this. They are a sickness that should be stamped out.

But, as I have said, the days ran together in the mines. We woke to labor and went to sleep with dread. Then, on a day that began like all the others, our routine changed. We were awakened with whips and fed as usual on onions and a thin gruel of bread, fish, and water. But we were not then driven immediately into the tunnels. Men began to sweat, fearful of the unknown. Had someone stolen a crust of bread perhaps? An entire chain was beaten for such a theft. Had someone spoken in an unguarded moment of escape? Men had died for that transgression.

The sweat ran down my own neck. I wondered if our attempts to break our chains had been found out. Around me, men panted harshly in the humid air. The dripping of slime from the stone roof marked the moments. We all started as a distant door banged aside and footsteps rang down the hall toward our cell. A slave whimpered and fell to his knees. Others cowered back against the walls, shoving against me.

Abruptly, the door to our cell flung back. Two guards came in, dragging a slim figure between them. Another whip slave stood behind them holding a crossbow. The guards went out after slinging down their bundle. I saw that it was a slave. She raised her head. Her eyes shone brown, soft and scared. Her head had been shaved. Her flesh was drawn tight over her ribs and blood streaked her body from the whip.

The guards had thrown a female slave among us. I had heard rumors that women who were not found pleasing were punished in this way. Several times I had heard slaves say that they wished a woman to be thrown to them. This sickened me.

The work slaves had been long, very long without the sight of a woman. This one was not clad in sumptuous silks. Gems did not flash at her ears and throat. But she looked and smelled like a female. A few pushed forward. Someone laughed. It was he who had moments before been on his knees whimpering in fear. More of the men pushed forward. I knew what they intended. Devous, the Ebon Llurn, and Kreeg, the ex-gladiator, stalked at their head.

"No," I said.

They did not listen.

Again, I said, "No!" shouting now. I took a step forward.

Men pushed against me. I was shoved backward. "Wait your turn," one of them snarled.

I shoved him aside and went forward. Two slaves spun me away and I sprawled to the floor, my leg chains tripping me. I could not see what was happening through the packed mass of bodies but suddenly I heard the girl scream. Laughter followed, very ugly.

Heril shoved forward, disgust on his face as he tried to make his way through the mob. Vriun was with him, I noted, even though he was Kaldi and the slave girl Human. The guards continued to watch, doing nothing. They too laughed. The girl sobbed brokenly.

I thought of my mother then, and of my sisters. I thought of Rannon and of the girl there before me. Anger surged behind my eyes. I reached down and grasped my leg irons and, in a fit of rage and frustration, snapped the links that had been weakened by constant scraping.

I straightened up, surged forward. Slaves barred the way. I hurled them aside. Devous and Kreeg had their hands on the girl, forcing her against the wall. She struggled vainly. I grabbed Kreeg and spun him around. I slipped one foot between his leg irons and put him down.

Devous turned, swung hard at me with his wrist chains looped together. I caught them in my left hand. They lashed about my forearm, numbing it with pain, but I was not thinking, not feeling, only reacting. I jerked the Llurn forward and got hold of him. And I broke his neck.

"Your back!" Vriun shouted.

I turned in time to catch Kreeg's charge. He hit me in the chest with his head, smashing me against the wall, but my muscles were hardened with labor and I did not lose my air. He drove short jabs to my ribs that I was just able to catch on my arms. His bullet skull butted up under my chin, but I was taller than he and the blow did not have the effect he wished. Clearly, though, this Kreeg had experience at close fighting with his fists.

I raised my hands, giving the ex-gladiator a free punch to my side, but then hammered down with both elbows into his shoulders and spine. And again. His muscles knotted with pain and I shoved him away from me. Another slave took a swing at me and Heril thumped him once behind the ear with the heavy manacle of his wrist chains and knocked him out cold.

But the Koro could not get through the crowd to Kreeg. That one was like a bull charging. I heard the roar of the slaves and guards and it was easy to imagine myself a matador and Kreeg really a bull. He came for me, taking short choppy steps to avoid tangling his chains. I had the advantage of him there, for my legs were free.

I slipped his rush, hurling him into the wall. He caromed off and charged again. I put a knee into his chest, missing the stomach where I had aimed. The blow jarred. I tried to get my hands around his neck but they slipped on the thick muscle there and on the sweat beaded on his flesh.

He lunged at me. I could not dodge him in the close confines of the cell. We clinched. He tried to bear-hug me and I broke it. Then he spiked a thumb at my eye and gouged only a cheek as I jerked my head aside. A blow aimed at my groin slid off a hip instead. And he was open for a moment. I punched him twice in the face and the second blow crossed his eyes.

He took a wild swing at me and missed. I punched him again and then looped my wrist chains over the back of his shaved head and jerked him forward into a knee. Cartilage crunched brutally in his nose. I pushed him up and shoved him into a wall. He struck it hard and sat down with a loud "oomph." He did not get up.

I spun and glanced at the others. "Touch her and I'll kill you," I told them. "We will be men, not animals."

I do not know why they did not walk over me. They had the numbers but I think they lacked the guts. They backed away, cowed.

The guards were not cowed. They carried whips and crossbows and did not fear an unarmed slave. No doubt they had handled such before. They rushed into the cell.

One struck me with a whip. It was a mistake. I had almost mastered my rage but under the lash it broke free again. I took the whip away from him and threw it aside. He backed away.

"Kill him!" he ordered the crossbowman. The weapon snarled as it cocked.

I had just said to the slaves that we would not be animals, but I was scarcely a man at that moment. I crouched, preparing to dodge the bolt when it was fired, and as if by accident Vriun stumbled into the bowman. The mechanism released. The quarrel flashed by my head and screeched off the stone wall, striking Devous's dead body. I launched myself from the crouch.

One of the whip slaves did not move fast enough and I

caught him about the waist and shoulders, lifting him over my head before slamming him down across a knee. He screamed once as his spine snapped. The work slaves, frustrated and angry, emboldened by seeing a guard killed, surged forward over the remaining guards and tore them to shreds.

I returned to the girl whose appearance had started all this carnage, through no fault of her own, and steadied her on her feet. Heril brought over a guard's buff tunic, which she took to cover her nakedness despite its scarlet stains.

Glancing about, I found the slaves staring at us with predatory eyes, their Khi awakened. I put a look on my face that said, "come if you dare." Heril was with me, his hands bloody, and Vriun took up the fallen crossbow and came to stand beside us. We were three tough men looking at them.

They had not attacked us before and they did not now. Their stares weakened and they glanced away. Kreeg staggered to his feet. I expected a fight to come from him, so when his pupils focused he found me glaring at him in readiness. He glared back a moment but there seemed almost a grudging respect on his face. He looked away, but I noted that he did not lower his gaze.

Pointedly, I looked toward the door of our cell. It stood open. The slaves followed that look and something very strange happened to their eyes and their backs. The former cleared and the latter straightened. Yet, no one moved. Their eyes flicked from the doorway to the three of us standing before them, then back to the doorway again. Men licked dry lips. Still, they did not move. It seemed they waited for something.

I passed the girl to Vriun and took up one of the short, metal headed staves the guards used to control recalcitrants.

"We all go together," I said.

The slaves—ex-slaves—nodded. How many times, I thought, had I been one or the other already on Talera? How many more times could I repeat the experience before it killed me?

CHAPTER TWENTY

A MEETING IN THE TUNNELS

We went out the door and turned to the left, moving deeper into the tunnels. I knew in which direction lay the surface but had no intention of going there just yet. We had come to fetch the Koro and I could not leave that task un-done. Too, there remained the possibility that my brother was here somewhere, and there were many other slaves in the mines who deserved a chance at freedom, some four thousand in all.

It was unclear how many men Rathgar had available to him. I had never observed more than fifty or so guards, but I assumed there were more. The mines were vast. Behind me stood eighteen men. Poor odds, it would seem. Still, I felt that we could take the whip slaves if we moved swiftly and swallowed them in bite-size pieces, our numbers growing as theirs lessened.

And there seemed little alternative. Hiding in the mines and trying to free the slaves slowly would not work. We had no food, almost no weapons, and no form of support. The advantages in such a war would lie with Rathgar, who could easily obtain help from his Klar masters. Our best chance lay in speed and surprise.

We needed weapons, though, and that's where I headed. I knew an armory where there would be staves and lances, perhaps a few crossbows. There would be no swords because the only blades allowed in the mines belonged to Rathgar and a few of his immediate henchmen. But then, I had used staves and lances before and knew that many swordsmen disdained them without cause.

As for my plans after taking Rathgar? Well, I saw two possibilities. We could seize the mines, which should be relatively defensible, and attempt some negotiations. Or, we could storm up into Andertalen and attempt to hack our way free.

The first option seemed preferable on the surface but was perhaps untenable. Negotiations have to be made from a position of strength and we had little. The Klar could easily bludgeon us into submission by cutting off our food and water.

On the other hand, I ached at the thought of the good men who would die if we chose the second option. Four thousand beings tired of whips and beatings could raise quite a bit of hell with the Klar's orderly civilization, but it would not be easy to fight the pirates with nothing other than chains and what few armaments we could muster. To pick either option might prove disastrous. But at least the slaves would have had the choice. That choice would have to wait, though, until the mines were free.

Despite the goad of impatience that drove me, I forced myself to move cautiously at first as we slipped through the tunnels away from our cell. The men behind me would break if we were attacked now. They needed weapons to strengthen their spines and a little time to taste their freedom.

I watched the men almost as much as I watched the corridors through which we passed, and I saw some look askance at me as we turned away from the surface. But none spoke and I knew that they would follow me for now, until I made a mistake or showed weakness. Then they would tear me to pieces. I sent Vriun to the rear of the column with our crossbow, as much to watch the slaves as to check for guards.

Ah, to have men at your back who would as lief stick you as follow you. It is something to concentrate one's faculties, and damn scary too.

We soon left the slave quarters behind, having seen no one. Fortunately, all of those in this section of the cells had worked the same shift as our chain and all were in the mines along with their guards. Every minute that passed without discovery increased our chances, and our confidence.

We went along several corridors and up a short flight of rough stairs until we came to the passageway where the armory lay. We had just started up that tunnel when the sound of combat rolled down toward us. I told Heril to keep the others back while I took the crossbow and raced ahead for a look. A few quick turns brought me almost to the armory.

I stopped at the last corner, flattened myself to a wall, and peeked around. Whip slaves were dying in front of the chamber beyond, their killers dressed all in gray—gray cloaks, gray hoods, gray gloves, and gray masks covering their faces. Even as I watched, the last guard fell. Instantly, a half dozen of the attacking warriors rushed into the armory and began carrying out bundles of weapons. This, along with their slaughter of the whip slaves, indicated that these cloaked figures were no friends of the Klar.

Obvious, you say? Well, just so. And if they were foes of the Klar then maybe they would be our allies. My father always said that the best way to gain friends was to make enemies of the right people.

I stepped out from my corner and began to walk slowly up the hallway toward the gray-cloaks, prepared to run or fight but preferring alliance. Their raid had been well organized and they seemed disciplined. Such would be of great help in freeing the slaves. I was not dressed for the part of an envoy, what with my bloody rags and matted hair and beard, but they did not retreat. Their own hands dripped blood and they were not frightened.

One lean, wolfish warrior pushed through the others to confront me. He started to pull away his hood but the sound of moving feet and rattling weapons stopped him. Those sounds came down from the corridor I had just quitted.

I flattened against the wall and threw a glance in the direction of the sound, then stiffened further in surprise as Heril and Vriun and the others I'd left behind came into view. Mingled with them, as if with old chums, came more of the mysterious gray warriors. At their head walked a very slim figure holding a rapier in one hand. I could not take my eyes from this one. There was something familiar there.

The approaching group stopped short a few feet from

me. The other gray-cloaks came up from behind. Well, if they meant to take me I had little chance to escape. That was not their intent, however. The slender figure beside Heril reached up a gloved hand and pulled away mask and hood. Dark hair was shaken back from a beautiful face, thinner than I remembered. An eyebrow arched; lips curved in a half smile.

"Rannon!" I said, and leaped forward. I took her shoulders, hard. She did not wince and her smile broadened. "Rannon," I repeated.

Words surged up in me. There was much I wanted to say, but now was not the time. This corridor full of corpses was not the place. I forced my hands to release her and drop to my sides.

"We were just coming to fetch you," she said. "Apparently under the mistaken impression that you needed help."

"We?" I questioned.

"I've brought along a few friends," she said.

A large warrior pushed out of the crowd behind her and pulled away his mask. Rhandh bulked as huge as ever and a broadsword glittered diamond-bright in his fist. I noted that his shoulders were thrown back and that pride lived again in his face. He seemed genuinely glad to see me, and I was most happy to see him.

Rannon gestured behind me then, and I turned to see another familiar form pulling off his hood. Emerald skin flashed.

"Valyan," I gasped, as we locked hands. "We feared you dead. How...?"

"I would have been in here with you and Heril were it not for Jask," he said.

"Jask saved us all," Rannon added.

I started. "Jask! How is he involved in all this?"

"After the fight in the temple," Rannon said, "Rhandh and I tried to flee through the city. But the Klar had been aroused and many came up from the direction of the harbor, blocking our escape. We would have been quickly captured but Jask had followed us and he hid us out until the furor passed."

"And later," Valyan added, "after I was taken to have

153

my wounds treated, Jask saw to it that I...disappeared."

"All right, I'll ask," I said. "Why is Jask helping us?"

Rannon laughed. "I think I'll let *him* explain. He's here in the mines. We'll take you to him but we'd best be moving. Other guards will be stumbling upon our little battlefield soon. Too much ruckus and Rathgar will have to send for reinforcements. He won't want to for fear the Klar will remove him from his position. He's also a slave you know. He doesn't want to be returned to a work chain because the Klar think he can't do his duty, but he'll take the chance if he fears an uprising."

"He'll still be after us," I said. "And he'll know we're armed."

"Yes," Valyan agreed, "but he'll think we're *your* bunch and he won't worry overly much about a few renegade slaves."

I had not thought of that, but the emerald Llurn's words made sense and I nodded. Quickly then, we left that place. I drifted along beside Rannon. Mentally, I cursed the fate that had kept her here instead of seeing her safely out of danger, but another part of me thrilled to her presence.

"You said you were coming to free us. How did you know that we would not be sent to the mines at the regular time today?" I asked her.

"We didn't until almost the last minute. That's why we came too late to help you escape. A spy that we have among Rathgar's people only just got word to us. We immediately decided to hit the armory at the same time. That way it would look as if you had broken loose and then taken the armory as well. You and your group did half of our first job for us."

"Have you made no other strikes then?"

"Not yet," she replied. "We've been laying plans, bringing a few people into the mines at a time, laying up supplies, spying on Rathgar, and waiting for a chance to free you and Heril. We've had to move slowly. Rathgar has about four hundred guards, most of whom are likely to be fanatical fighters since losing would mean a death sentence at the hands of the other slaves."

"Four hundred guards!" I choked out.

154

"About that. Perhaps a few more. Why?"

"Nothing," I said. I was thinking of my plans to conquer the whip slaves piecemeal with my handful of followers. We would have been cut down almost immediately. Realizing the kind of fool that I am sometimes is excruciatingly painful.

I said nothing else for a bit and we went along in silence. I was content to walk beside Rannon, to know that Rhandh and Valyan were safe, and that other friends were with me. Rhandh. Valyan. Heril. Vriun. All were good men, even though none were quite Human. I only wished that Jedik were here. Thoughts of him brought a twinge.

Rannon's teasing voice broke the sudden dip in my mood. "Heril told me what happened when you escaped. I see you make a habit of rescuing ladies in distress. And I thought I was the only one you so troubled yourself over."

"Just trying to keep in shape in case you need rescuing again some time in the future," I joked back at her.

She looked at me from under dark lashes and smiled slightly. I felt my face growing warm and looked away, laughing a little to hide my discomfort. After a bit she reached up and squeezed my biceps with a slimly muscled hand. My head seemed very light. Incredibly, I felt almost like doing a jig down the corridor. I restrained myself.

It did not take long to leave the lava mines behind, and as the ruddy glow of the pit faded some of Rannon's guerillas fired torches to light our way. We moved into cooler tunnels that had never been worked, the remnants of magma vents that had died centuries ago. It was quiet in the near darkness, even the drip of water gone, and we walked along inside our own silences like ghosts.

I thought that we had been going upward for some time, and this was confirmed as the familiar blue glow of Andertalen returned to the walls. We soon came back into corridors that had been marked by tools, though our feet left scuff marks in dust that had long been undisturbed.

We stopped in a passage where recent trails marred the dust. Warriors in gray slipped around corners to keep watch. Rannon, Heril, Valyan, Rhandh, and I entered a small room at the end of a stone hall. A Klar stood behind a wooden ta-

155

ble within. It was alone, and as it turned I saw that it was Jask. He grinned. I raised a hand to him and he threw me a sword.

"Have you a taste for freedom, warrior?" he asked.

"You know that I do," I replied.

"Then it is yours."

"And what will it cost?"

"For your freedom? Nothing. But the freedom of others here in the mines may not be so cheaply purchased."

"Let's hear the point," I said.

"It is really quite simple," the Klar said.

"Go on."

"You saw the Thye Vessoth in the temple."

I nodded.

"I told you that my people had once thrown out their evil cult. It seems that it was not completely eradicated and that its head has risen again while I have been gone roving this past half a year. I must stomp on that head but I need help, the help of the slaves."

"I see," I said.

"I do not know how much you understand of our political system, but I will tell you enough so that you may realize why I wish to do this."

"All right," I said, "I'm listening."

The others listened also. For Heril as well as myself it would be the first time we had heard it.

"Our people have long been ruled by a council of priests," Jask began. "Now the council has been taken over by the Thye Vessoth. They have convinced the priests that Heshval and Vessoth are manifestations of the same deity. There is some precedence for this in our beliefs. They are often called the 'twins.'

"Too, I think there is more to it than that but I have not yet discovered what. The Thye Vessoth have taken over worship of both gods and have begun...sacrifices. It is their belief that enough blood offerings will free Vessoth from a prison that he was placed in long ago by an alliance of other gods.

"The sacrifice of Rannon was to have begun it all. She was especially chosen and their rage was great when you stole her away. That did not stop them, though, and in only a few months the sacrifices have increased. Now it is not only slaves who die, but Klar as well. Even women and children."

"And your people allow this?" Heril asked.

"Oh, there is grumbling. A lot of it. But the people fear the priests. And the clan nobility have too much invested in the present system to speak up. Besides, it is only the Keshaki, those who have no claims to clan, who are being sacrificed. They are the poor and powerless.

"I have mentioned them to you, Ruenn, before. I am one of them. We have no voice in our government and the Thye Vessoth have used this, playing up to the clans and the priests. The only strength of the Keshaki is in numbers, and I am not without influence among them. Many of them are prepared to fight to see things change. They will rise in revolt when I command, and I expect that many more, perhaps even among the clans, will join us as well once the fight is under way."

"You had better not count on that last," I said.

"I do not. That is why I need the slaves."

"How many Klar can you muster?" I asked.

"Close to five thousand. You know that we are primarily a sea power. We have no standing armies. The clans each have their own militias, but they are almost all Keshaki and I have the assurance of some of these that they will join us. I expect to have more such pledges soon.

"The only really powerful force that we will have to meet is the Priests' Guard. They are four thousand religious fanatics who are willing to die for their god. I fear we'll have to let them *all* die for their god. I don't think they will surrender. They are with the priests' council in Kwellarn the Lower, in the temple district.

"While the council is intact we cannot hope to win, but we cannot get at them while they are inside this district. It is walled and the Guard is strong enough to hold those walls against any number of attackers. We must lure the council out and the only thing likely to do that is a general revolt of the slaves. They have long feared such. That is a major reason for the existence of the Guard."

"How do you envision this rebellion?" I asked him.

"Well, the only organized force of slaves, or rather ex-slaves, is outside this room. They will have to be the core. Many were once fighting slaves, owned either by me or by others who are with me. I may be able to slip a few more in to you. We have also been in contact with the Emirian ship but I doubt that I can bring any of them into Andertalen. They will have to help us outside."

I nodded.

"As for the slaves in the mines," he continued, "I will leave the decision on how best to proceed up to you and the others. We can supply you with some weapons and with food. I will maintain contact with you by using some of my own slaves."

"You know, of course," I said, "that it is hard to overthrow a government backed by religion."

"Yes, but the majority of the people are rapidly becoming disillusioned with the Thye Vessoth and the sacrifices. Also," he smiled, "I have persuaded two priests, including a high priest, to sanction the revolt when it occurs."

"The high priest would not happen to be called Relic would he?" I asked.

"Why yes," Jask answered, surprised. "How did you know?"

"It was he who sentenced Heril and I to the mines. Yet, I thought then that he did not much care for the Thye Vessoth."

"You are right. He is harsh but honorable, and he hates what the servants of Vessoth have done, and are doing."

"What of the vaunted sorcerous powers of the Thye Vessoth?" Heril asked.

Jask's savage face wrinkled in a frown. "Aye, there's a rub. They'll use their magic if they can but they are not nearly as powerful as they would have people think. It takes them time to make their preparations. We'll have to strike quickly. The one we have to watch is their leader. He seldom leaves the temple district but his powers appear real at least. His name is Nethcormundis."

I frowned. *Nethcormundis?* Where had I heard that word before? It came to me suddenly. *Nethcormundis!* The Thye Vessoth I'd seen on Earth had shouted that word just as his sphere gate exploded. It had not been a curse or a prayer as I had supposed, but the name of the beast's master. It seemed I owed a score to this Nethcormundis, this sorcerer. But before I killed him I would ask him some questions about my brother and my crew.

Something Jask had mentioned about the sacrifices came back to haunt me then. He had said that the Thye Vessoth were offering much blood to free their god from some prison. Had my crew been stolen for such a purpose? I could not think it.

And what of Bryce? He had not been taken with the others but could the lizard priests have gotten their hands on him still? Well, surely the sorcerer would know. I smiled grimly to myself, then turned back to the business at hand.

"What do the slaves get out of this revolt?" I asked Jask.

"Their freedom," the Klar said.

"Who will grant it?"

"I will," he said. "When I set at the head of a *new* council, a free council in which all Klar are represented. Then will the slaves in the mines be freed."

"All the slaves, period." I said.

The pirate smiled. "I expected some such demand," he said. "And you have me at a disadvantage. We must have your help. I promise to do as you wish, but I will have to move slowly. I do not want a second civil war on my hands so soon after the first."

"Agreed," I said. "Also, we here will crush Rathgar and then let out word that a revolt is underway. However, we will have to let the enemy come to us in the mines. Untrained as we are, and undisciplined, we could not hope to meet even militia in the open."

"I understand," Jask replied. "You need only draw them out. And you will. But when we fall on their rear you will have to attack from the front."

"Of course," I said.

"Are you sure the council will come out?" Heril asked.

"Some will, and as for the rest it doesn't really matter as long as the defenders are out. We can take the temple district if the Priests' Guard is gone. And they will have to come. They're the only force that can deal with a slave uprising."

"How will we know friends from foes?" I asked.

"The Guard, you will know. They wear black leathers and carry black shields with a golden fang in the center. The clans also have insignia on their shields. The Keshaki do not."

"But not all the Keshaki will rise with you," I said.

"True, but I've thought of that. I proposed to the council, and it was accepted, that certain of the Keshaki troops be allowed to paint two black stripes on their shields as a sign of their complete loyalty to the priesthood. All of these are ours."

I laughed at the irony. "Then we must make plans," I said.

Jask smiled broadly. "We will. But first let us celebrate our alliance."

He reached into a bag on the table and drew out two bottles of crimson wine and several brass goblets. I knew the wine from the maroon labels that adorned the bottles. It is called She-ashin and is often used on Talera to seal bargains. It is not made by the Klar but by the Threshians. This particular stash must have been liberated by Klar pirates from a Threshian vessel.

The cups were filled and handed around. I raised mine and drank, wondering if it were an omen that the wine was the color of blood.

CHAPTER TWENTY-ONE

REVOLT

Rathgar and his people searched for us during the following weeks but we easily avoided them in the maze of tunnels and mines that lay beneath Andertalen. They soon gave up, failing to realize that we were anything more than a disorganized handful of starving, escaped slaves. For our part, we made no more attacks on armories or attempts to free men. We did not wish to arouse the Syber to greater effort.

In the meantime, in the less frequented tunnels, we laid our plans carefully. Reinforcements trickled in to us in a slow but steady stream. The majority of these had once been fighting slaves, or rahnvin, and their skills made them worth far more than their numbers would suggest. We were armed as well, with crossbows, lances, and swords that Jask or his people smuggled in for us. A few of us even had shields and a bit of mail to cover our nakedness.

In our planning we drew maps to study the corridors down which we would attack and the strongholds that would have to be reduced. Heril and Valyan organized strike forces to free selected chains of Koro and Nakscherii (the Green Llurns), those whom we could trust to maintain discipline. We would need them to augment our numbers during the revolt and we thought it folly to free all the slaves at once. Overwhelmed with their new liberty, they would pour out into Andertalen in an unarmed and undisciplined mass that would be easily scythed down. Our cause would be lost.

Such a flood of free men was much what I had planned

before I learned of Jask's "revolt." But now we had better options. We wanted a coup to gain the slaves' attention. Then we could free them one chain at a time and put them into troops that had already been organized on paper. The officers would come from among ourselves or the rahnvin.

As I say, we needed a coup. We planned one. It was the habit of Rathgar to watch the labor of the slaves from a perch high above the central lava pit. A rock chimney that ran up behind this shelf brought cool, sweet air down from Andertalen, and there the Syber and his guards could sit at their ease and see men dying below them.

The ledge hung in clear sight of the hundreds of slaves who labored in the central chasm at all times. There was even a bronze gong that Rathgar used to call for attention when a proclamation was to be read or a penalty to be carried out. A common punishment was to hurl the prisoner off into the lava.

We determined to seize this ledge from Rathgar and his cronies in plain view of the slaves below. When those hundreds joined us we would be well on our way to getting out of the mines. I did not doubt that we could take the guards. Many of us were skilled with weapons while Rathgar's men had been chosen more for their cruelty and brutality than for their martial expertise.

The only question in my mind was whether or not I could take Rathgar. He had been rahnvin, and though I had some little claim to that title myself I had never fought for blood and glory in the arenas, or for breath and life in the pits. Rathgar had. He'd been, I had learned, the most famous gladiator in the Klar world before pride brought him low; he'd killed hundreds.

Within the mines, leadership belonged to me. It was Jask's idea and none of the others would let me put it aside. I saw the faith in their eyes and knew that I had to be worthy of it. But, while those with us now might believe, the remainder of the slaves knew nothing of me. I would have to earn their faith.

Men generally follow those who prove to them that they are strong enough to lead. No one wants to follow a committee to war. They want a leader, a warlord, or as they say on

Talera, a Khisan. I was no warlord. I was only a man, not particularly large, not particularly bright. The only way I could think of to show the slaves that I had what it took to get them out of the mines was to defeat Rathgar in single combat while they watched. They feared the Syber. They feared his whip, and his sword, and his wrath. They would follow the one who beat him. At least that was my hope.

I knew how much I had developed as a swordsman since coming to Talera. I knew I was good. Well, I'd had good teachers. But was I good enough to take the Syber? Those beasts are stronger than a man. They are swift and they have four arms. They have a tail that is tufted like that of a lion and the tuft conceals a sharp barb that contains poison, though Humans—who developed under a different sun—are immune to it. I was not immune to a barb in the eye, however, or steel through the vitals. And the word kept coming back to me, Rathgar had been a rahnvin.

Rhandh suggested that we arrow Rathgar down when we attacked. When I vetoed that idea he asked that he be allowed the pleasure of the fight. Undoubtedly, both his suggestions were wise ones. But *I* had to lead the slaves.

I wondered why I should lead. Others here had greater experience. Yet, I think I knew at least part of the reason. There is a look that I can put on my face and a tone that can ache in my voice, and in seeing me and hearing me men will follow. I do not know why this should be. I had never had cause to give it much thought before. Nor did I now really, for there were many things to be done. But at last the time for deeds was upon us.

On the day set for the revolt we put on our gray cloaks and buckled on our swords. We loaded copper-headed quarrels into the crossbows and slung iron shields over our backs. Nearly fifty of us waited at a mere wide space in the tunnels, and others, perhaps a hundred more, were already in position for the attack.

We stood quiet in our thoughts, with no need for speech. Everyone knew their duties and we moved off purposefully. Some, under Heril or Valyan, went to free as many chains of Koro and Nakscherii as they could. Others went to strike at armories and places where routes led to the surface. We did not want word of the uprising leaking out until we were ready.

A dozen beings, Rhandh included, followed me. We were rahnvins all and there were as many kinds of weapons among us as there were men. I held a heavy saber and had a short sword slung over my shoulder beneath my shield. Rhandh carried a saber that was twin to my own and a six inch length of steel was strapped to his tail. Others came armed with rapiers, or tulwars, or war axes, or black-hafted lances. We all carried daggers.

There would be ten men with Rathgar, or so it was habitually. They would be armed primarily with whips and staves and broadswords. It would be their brute strength against our speed and skill. I felt sorry for them, all that is except for Rathgar. He was a different matter. I considered him then. I held a picture of him in my mind. Everywhere our margin of advantage was small or nonexistent. At any point our plan could break down. I thought of none of this. I thought of Rathgar. Everything else was out of my hands.

We crept stealthily through the corridors toward our destination, our gray cloaks blending imperceptibly with the stone of the walls. We carried no torches and needed none, for the ruddy light of the lava pit guided our way, the same light that had watched over our slavery such a short time before.

Soon, we reached the path that led up to Rathgar's Perch, as the slaves called the ledge whereupon the Syber watched them work. Two guards warded its foot. Two of our rahnvin were bowmen. They drew now and loosed, using longbows made from the yellow wood of the traen-tha tree and dark arrows fletched with the steel-blue feathers of the mountain tull. Their aim went true and the guards fell, dying silently with arrows through their throats. I did not like this striking from ambush, but the lives of too many innocents were at stake to allow a warning to get out now. We hid the corpses in a side tunnel and the bowmen took their places. The rest of us moved on.

It took only a few minutes to reach the heights of the ledge. There were no other guards and Rathgar's ten men did not even glance our way, so confident were they in their power. We threw off our cloaks and stalked forward proudly. Somewhere among us a sword rattled against a shield and they turned. They saw us.

They were on the ledge, we in the tunnel. They could not escape except through us and we had no intention of allowing that. But they were not yet ready to run, and they drew their weapons. The light of the pit flickered luridly along the steel.

One of the whip slaves sounded a gong, a call for help no doubt. I did not think it would come. Our strike groups in the tunnels would see to that. All the gong did was attract the attention of the slaves below and thus play into our hands. Those workers lifted their heads and curved spines, and arched their eyes up to where the battle was joined that would decide their fate.

We rushed forward, ripping brands from sheathes. They roared to meet us, nowhere else for them to go. They were bully boys and bravos, but they fought. Cornered, they turned loose all the viciousness of their natures.

They met us in the tunnel and our charge carried them back onto the ledge. Razor edged steel slashed and parried and drew blood, screaming. Whips cracked and raped skin from bones. A man died under my feet.

I fought my way toward Rathgar. His four hands were full of blades, full of short swords and daggers and a broadsword gripped in one massive gray fist. He dismembered two of my men before I kicked a dead guard away from me and reached to tear him down.

We engaged, whirling. A dagger grated off my targe. His barbed tail whipped at my legs. I avoided it to the right, dropping my shield to cover my chest against another stroke. Around me, the fighting raged at its height. Soon it would die down. I only hoped that I would not die with it.

Rathgar hurled a dagger at me that clattered off my shield. I dodged in close, too close for him to ply his giant broadsword easily. He retreated, holding my point at bay on his own steel. Again his tail reached for me. I stomped at it and he jerked it back. My saber slid lightly along his lower left arm, bringing blood and sending his other dagger flying. He side-armed his broadsword and I leaped back, and he

165

took the chance to pluck up a shield that had been dropped by one of my men. He kicked the body at me.

I felt the red sparks leap in my eyes and a flash of chill went up my neck. In that anger I hurled myself on him, driving him back. He parried furiously, then riposted, his blade sliding over my shoulder as I went under it. I thrust my shield into his chest, forcing him further back, and went with him. He caught himself and held, then hurled me off. His broadsword glanced from my shield, numbing the arm beneath. By the Lord, he was strong.

I waved my sword in his face, dropped it down and went in low. He caught the thrust and drove it aside. I danced away from his counter. We fought very near the cliff's edge, skipping and leaping about as if a two hundred foot drop into boiling magma did not lie at our heels. Around us there were the shouts of straining men; from below came the roar of flames and the screams of slaves. All of it seemed muffled, lost in the distance and the fog of battle.

The Syber whipped his tail at me between his own legs, and this time it caught at my ankle, jerking me forward. I slid to both knees to avoid a killing stroke, but I missed the taloned foot that crushed into my chest, hurling me onto my back. I rolled away from another kick and batted a sword strike away with the shield, the tip of the blade ripping up sparks by my head.

Rathgar stomped down at my jugular and I dropped sword and targe to catch his foot. I held him for a moment, all of his weight poised above my throat. Somehow I found the strength to throw him off. He staggered but did not fall. Yet that brief respite allowed me time to scoop up a blade and shield and climb to my feet.

Immediately, Rathgar moved in. Once more he struck at me with his tail. The barb ripped my thigh, then again. Blood ran but the barb did not go deep. I watched Rathgar's eyes, as black as obsidian marbles, unreadable. I slid my leg forward a bit, exposing it to his tail, hoping that it would seem weak. I did not have to fake a tremor. The tail licked out, as if on its own. At the same time the Syber swung hard with his broadsword.

I ducked behind my shield, catching the falling blow on

the rim. The rim caved in but clutched at his brand for just an instant. I ignored the sword, trusting in the well-tempered metal of the shield, and hacked downward and to the side with my own blade. It sliced through the Syber's tail just back of the barb. That tuft of hair spun out over the ledge and fell into space.

I powered up from my crouch, spinning, and kicked out with a booted foot. It caught Rathgar's shield as he pulled back, smashing it up into him. He stood too near the edge. He teetered there for a moment, hanging by his heels. His eyes looked at me and for the first time there seemed emotion in their depths, a plea perhaps.

I leaped forward, groping for his hand. His feet slipped before I could reach him and all I could do was stand on the edge and watch him fall. He had not screamed when I'd taken his tail. He did not now. A hundred feet down he hit the wall and bounced out and away. He did not make much of a splash in the lava.

Silence held around me and I realized that the fight was over for Rathgar's men as well as for himself. I stood on the edge of the chasm. My gaze swept out, seeing five hundred slaves watching us, without movement. A few guards still huddled among them but they could do little. Their comrades would already be our prisoners. I looked down and raised the bloody sword and dented shield.

"Slaves," I shouted. My voice carried easily, echoing in the caverns, in the broken tunnels where men had toiled for decades. "Slaves. Hear me. If you would be free. Hear me."

I spoke to them at length then. I do not remember what I said. I think there were words about liberty and honor, about glory, such things as you say to men when you know that many of them will soon die. It is hard to command men.

They listened, without sound, to every word I uttered. And when I finished they raised their chains and their voices and the sound of freedom roared up through the mines like the rushing of a great river. A beast was awakened. Now I had to control it.

CHAPTER TWENTY-TWO

AN ARMY MARCHES

Victory reaped a whirlwind, and revealed a kaleidoscope of races, personalities, and conflicts beneath the ragged uniformity of the slaves. Those slaves, all four thousand of them in the mines, were freed a chain at a time and assigned to troops already laid out for them. It was an impressive display as we had drawn it, and now the troops filled out with beings of flesh and blood and they were far more impressive.

As of yet, however, only about half of our forces were armed. Rathgar's storerooms had yielded only a few hundred lances and crossbows, and weapon shipments from Jask had come in slowly and were inadequate for our needs.

Lack of cold steel was perhaps our most urgent problem, but not the only one by far. Food was plentiful, having been stockpiled in the mines for some time, but water was precious. In addition, some of the slaves we freed proved to be hardened criminals, sold to the Klar as punishment for their predations. A band of these slipped away into Andertalen. I would have been happy to see them go but they broke into an armory before fleeing and escaped with some of our hoarded store of weapons.

There were, as well, battles between various races or creeds to be broken up, for even in the midst of our collective need there was still prejudice. I busted some heads. Curiously, Kreeg, the ex-gladiator who I'd fought in our cell before our escape, always seemed to be there when I needed someone to back up my own muscles.

Others among the slaves were afraid and needed their

spines stiffened. Well, that was understandable. But even more seemed eager to come to hand-strokes with their former captors. These, I had to convince to wait. I was harsh, autocratic, uncompromising, all of the things that I hate. But I felt it to be necessary.

Ah, there's the crux. Perhaps all tyrants feel their commands to be necessary. I do not know. I know only that we came very close to losing control of the revolt and seeing the slaves roar up to the surface in a red mist. We held them back but it was a near thing. I could not have achieved it without Rannon, Valyan, Heril, Rhandh, and Vriun, among others. Together we sorted things out. Perhaps on Earth it could never have been done, but Talera is a warlike world and many of the slaves had been soldiers at one time or another. Oh yes, we sorted things out, but we got little sleep for our pains.

I saw the least of Rannon, though it was her that I most wished to see. Many in the mines had been broken in body and in Khi by the savage labor and the hopelessness. Rannon took it upon herself to see to these. With the help of Vriun, who had been trained as a physician, and others of the Koro and Kaldi, she moved the suffering into the cooler tunnels, tended their hurts, and even managed to fix them decent meals.

I spoke to her only when she came to give me some of her strength. Even exhausted, with dirt on her face and tear stained eyes, she was beautiful. It hurt to turn away from her and plan for war when all I wished to do was hold her hand and find some quiet place to rest.

But there was to be no rest for any of us yet. At mid-morning on the sixth day we received word that the Priests' Guard was marching. Well, we had expected it, even solicited it. Rhandh and Valyan had seen to that by using their strike forces to crush a few Klar outposts, informing the slavers rather abruptly that something had changed in their homeland.

Rhandh struck an armory near the outskirts of Kwellarn the Lower. He lost some men but returned with stolen wagons loaded with badly needed weapons. Valyan's men hit an encampment where tasabers were kept. Once mounted, they split into small raiding parties whose duty was to sow confusion by running off herds and burning outlying steadings. Another of their jobs was to report on Klar troop movements, and it was one such scout who let us know that the slavers marched. He told us also that several Thye Vessoth traveled with the columns. I did not like a bit of that.

As soon as I learned of the Klar advance, I set the majority of our forces to strengthening some barricades in front of the mines that Heril and his Koro had begun. The entrance to the lava pits lay on a slight rise above the surrounding country. On this slope we piled up loose walls of lava blocks that had been stored in the tunnels for later use in Klar buildings. There was grim satisfaction in knowing that at least some of our labor of past weeks would be used to defend us against the Klar.

On the evening of the sixth day I went up to inspect the barricades. Five hundred of our best guarded them and they were stronger than I had hoped. In front of the rough wall, covering the slope below, we had placed sharpened stakes to impede an enemy charge. These were really meant for cavalry, of which the Klar had none, but they might slow a foot advance a little.

After finishing my inspection, I crawled up on the highest point of the rocks and looked east to where lay Kwellarn and the priests' army. I saw no sign of them and had not really expected to. No more than twenty verlangs (about thirty miles) separated the city from the mines and a warrior on a horse or tasaber could have covered that distance in less than a day. A marching column of soldiers moves as slow as their slowest troop, however, and could not.

The Guard was supposed to have left the city around midday. That meant they would have to spend at least one night on the road. I guessed that they would come up to us on the afternoon of the next day, but they would be tired. It seemed likely that they would wait until another dawn to launch their attack.

I wondered where Jask was and let that worry me for a bit. Some Klar rebels should be marching within the unsuspecting ranks of the priests' army, but most would be moving with Jask to come up behind the enemy. According to the plan, Jask would advance on the Priests' Guard as they faced the slaves outside the mines. The Guard would have to wheel to face the new threat, and after they had engaged with Jask's troops the slaves under me would strike them from the rear.

Simultaneously, or at least close in time to our joining battle, rebel forces would strike at the heart of both Kwellarns, the Upper and the Lower. The surface forces would have Jedik's Emirians with them, while Relic, a high priest of Heshval, would lead the attack in Andertalen. Strongholds would be isolated while the insurrectionists fought for the support of the mass of uncommitted Klar.

It all had to be timed properly. If anything went wrong, if any of the Klar rebels deserted us or if they struck too soon, then we here at the mines would die. We could do nothing but wait and hope, and fondle our steel.

I ordered more men to be brought up to support the barricades and waited for night to fall. When it came at last I saw many flames rising where Valyan and his men harassed and impeded the enemy approach. The fires burned out toward morning. I hoped that was not a bad sign.

Dawn came late, as if clouds of smoke obscured some of the mineral light of the cavern walls and ceiling. With the dawn, however, came good news, a messenger from Jask informing us that his forces were moving and would arrive on time. A cheer went up along the line of ex-slaves as I read that news to them. It seemed ironic that they cheered word of marching Klar.

The priests' army marched as well, though, and toward late afternoon they loomed up out of a pall of dust that followed them. There were more of them than I expected, or had hoped. Besides a majority of the Priests' Guard, some three thousand of them, there were several thousand other Klar, both Keshaki and clan warriors. Through a spyglass, I estimated around seven thousand enemy in all. Many of the Keshaki, I hoped, would be on our side when the killing started.

Now I really began to sweat. The rest of our forces, save for a small reserve, hurried to the surface. We had about twenty-eight hundred effectives, but many were undisciplined and could not be counted on if we started to lose the fight.

When the Klar host was within half a verlang, I went and stood where I could gain the best view of their approach. They came down on us in a moving wall of steel and flesh, and for a moment I feared that they meant to overwhelm us at once. I gave swift orders to prepare, but—at the last second it seemed—the enemy veered aside and halted a few hundred yards from our lines. Our barricades seem to have surprised them.

We exchanged arrows, though only a few were fired on our part because we had few to begin with and none to waste. I only ordered some of our archers to shoot in hopes that it would draw return fire. This worked well. They hurled sheaves of arrows at us in response to every one we shot at them. Few of their darts found a mark because our people lay well hidden behind stacks of lava blocks, but we ended up with many new arrows for our own quivers.

Soon the rain of arrows faded and a new rain began, of water from the sky. It was not time for the periodic drizzle that falls in Andertalen to come down, but I suppose the rising smoke had triggered the release early. Beneath the rain, hurriedly, the Klar threw up a camp of black tents, as black as the night that soon fell. Fires were lit among them, protected from the wet by metal shields. Occasionally, sentries moved between the fires and us, casting giant shadows. The remainder of their camp slept, or seemed to. Our men, too, tried to get some rest.

I was bone weary myself but nervousness and excitement kept me striding back and forth behind our lines, waiting, watching. So it came about that I was among the first to hear the chant of harsh voices and see the swell of emerald flames from the heart of the Klar encampment.

The Thye Vessoth!

I did not believe in sorcery, I told myself. There had to be some reasonable explanation for the seemingly magical powers of the lizard priests. But it had been in the presence of such flames that my Earthly crew had been taken from me, and I knew, sorcery or no, there might be enough power in that camp to destroy us before we even had a chance to

172

come to blows with our enemy.

I awakened those near me and in a few moments the word spread and the length of the barricade roused and made ready for whatever would come. Rannon walked from her place to stand beside me, and would not go back into the tunnels when I would have sent her. She carried with her a sword.

"What is it?" she asked.

I pointed below to the dancing green darkness and told her my fears. She said nothing, just stood there sharing those fears with me.

Was it a minute or an hour before it came upon us? I do not know. It began as a brittle howling, faint as the least wind. But there was no wind. The sound grew louder and more shrill, and then the air around us *did* begin to moan. There is never much wind in Andertalen but it was here to-night. And it was cold.

From below our position, from the direction of the Klar camp, a gray fog came rolling toward us, driven hard by a stiff breeze. In the fog there lived something that reached out and...touched us. I felt an obscene caress and shook my head, trying to rid myself of a feeling like ants digging just below the skin. Beings began to whimper in fear, then in terror. Rannon shivered and moved closer beneath my arm.

A smell like the stench of bloating corpses rolled over us, and wicked whispers murmured tauntingly in our ears. A man beside me stood and tried to run. I caught him and hurled him back to his post. Another fell to his knees and began tearing at his face. I jerked him to his feet and slapped him twice. He caught himself.

Others began inching backward now, but the Llurns, and Koro, and more among them stood firm. Beside me, a sav-agely scarred Nokarran with gin-colored eyes scratched his red whiskers and looked bored. I went to stand on the height of our barricade, Rannon beside me, and the men, shamed by seeing a woman face what they feared, returned slowly to their posts.

After that the fog went as swiftly as it had come, and the touch of evil went with it. Only slowly did our heartbeats return to normal, and few among us got any more sleep that night. I could not understand why the sorcerous attack had been stopped. Why had the Thye Vessoth not tried harder to destroy us? I said as much to Rannon.

"I think you overestimate their strength," she said. "If they could have destroyed us they would have, but they do not possess that much power. At least not now."

"I do not understand how they have any power," I said.

"It is through those emerald wands they possess. Each of them has been touched to a toir'in-or and used to draw off and encapsulate some of its power."

"I have heard of the toir'in-or," I said. "Jedik told me of them. Still, I do not understand how it is that they work."

"From what I know of sorcery," she said, "which is admittedly very little, the crystalline structure of the toir'in-or amplifies mental energy just as a theater can be constructed to amplify a singer's voice. The toir'in-or are too powerful to be used for most purposes, however. Instead, other crystals, like the Thye Vessoth wands, are placed in close proximity to the milkstone and their structures are realigned. This drains the toir'in-or but each jewel can be used to empower a number of wands, which are safer to use."

"Why is that?"

"They are just not as powerful. It takes years to master the disciplines needed to control the milkstones and even adepts have been driven mad by their unfettered use. The wands have little power when compared with the toir'in-or. They can be used to work such tricks as we just witnessed, and perhaps a bit more in the hands of an adept. Even this, as you see, requires time and preparation. And I am told the practitioner is drained of much strength. The wizards must only have hoped to panic us and keep us from sleep. They will probably try again in the morning before their attack."

"These adepts you speak of," I said. "Is the Thye Vessoth who is called Nethcormundis among them?"

"He is," she said. "I saw him once while I was a prisoner. Before you and the others rescued me. His body is crippled, his legs in metal braces, but he exudes destruction does that one. Thank the gods that his injuries prevent him from joining those below."

A shudder swept me. It might have been a lingering caress from the wizard's cold wind that caused it. At least that was what I told myself. But even then I knew I was lying. I was afraid.

CHAPTER TWENTY-THREE

RED SWORDS AT DAWN

The rain ceased during the night and the morning came in blueness. With it there arose green fire from the direction of the Klar camp. The men around me stirred, uneasy, as much from the sorcery they expected as from the sight of the Priests' Guard and the clan militias lining up for an on-slaught. I nocked an arrow. Other hands, too, tightened on weapons.

But before the fog—or something worse—could roll upon us, we heard shouts and a clatter of confusion in the enemy formations. The emerald lights died. Behind them, the Guard and the priests had seen movement, coming swiftly. I smiled.

Jask's warriors must have marched part of the way in the dark and I wondered how that had been accomplished in the almost total blackness of the Andertalen night. I was happy it had been though. The ebon shields of the Priests' Guard spun to meet this new foe, leaving squares of clan mi-litia and Keshaki to face the slaves. The Keshaki stood on the right, the clans on the left. The latter opened up at us with arrows and the Keshaki soon followed suit, though sporadi-cally. We held our own fire, waiting.

Jask's army numbered about four thousand Klar. They were strung out a bit from their march but quickly formed up. On the troop's flanks rode small bands of cavalry. These were Valyan's men, now linked up with our allies. They were all mounted on swift tasabers and wasted no time in rushing in to the attack, in part to allow Jask the time to or-

176

ganize his forces.

Neither Valyan nor his men were true cavalrymen—there are few on Talera—and the tasabers they rode were not trained coursers. The whole mass of mounted men came boiling up to the Klar lines, spitting quarrels and arrows and lances, and taking hits of their own. Tasabers went down, shrieking, and men rolled free or lay smashed and broken. Here and there a black-clad slaver fell, but the sally left little impression on the ranked files of the Guard. It did give the rebels time to gather themselves.

Jask was no general. He spent no time in preliminary maneuvers but hurled his entire army forward as soon as they were ready, keeping only a small reserve that directly surrounded him. The Priests' Guard came stalking forward to meet the assault, moving ponderously. The two forces crashed together in the open and the dust and the dull blue light.

Jask's Klar swarmed forward, hacking and slicing, rapidly losing any semblance of discipline. The Priests' Guard were quickly enveloped but moved on, like a ship cutting through the froth of stormy waves.

The militia hesitated for a crucial moment, not knowing in which direction to turn. Just as they decided to help the black guards, the Keshaki on the right, those who bore two stripes of jet on the lacquered surface of their shields, turned in a tight formation and rolled up the militia's line, driving it into the back of the priests' army.

At the same time, Valyan, on his own initiative, led a thrust into the other flank of the militia. The clan troops were undoubtedly brave but they had never faced a cavalry attack before. Even Valyan's few mounted warriors, poorly armed and disciplined as they were, raised havoc in the enemy lines.

Assailed from two sides, the militia broke. But the Priests' Guard did not break. The momentum of the cavalry was lost by the time they came within striking range of the Guard, and those black-clad professionals took a moment to stomp on Valyan's brave warriors, hurling them back with such brutal losses that it finished them for the war.

Jask's men had regrouped a bit in the respite, but the

black guards were soon on them again and the battle teetered on the brink for a moment. Just as it seemed that the waves of Jask's attack would break on the beach of their foes, I drew my sword and screamed a charge. Over two thousand men who had once been slaves swarmed over the lava barricades we had erected and roared down the hill. The battle raged only two hundred yards away and we ran the entire distance.

The militia had been separated entirely from the Priests' Guard and a leader had come forth among them. By the spiral and hawk shield I knew him to be Truen. But I had no time for him now. He had rallied the clans momentarily against the Keshaki, but he was between us and the Guard and it was the Guard we wanted. We smashed into him and then smashed over him in a crashing wave, rolling the clan warriors under. Jask, seeing our attack committed, hurled in his reserve, and in a moment the field had become an imbroglio of surging flesh and steel, all of it assaulting the formation of the priests' fanatical warriors.

We broke their outer line, though many of us did not survive it, and reached the center of their formation to find the Thye Vessoth and several Klar priests. Sorcerers or no, they died as easily as men when steel went through them. And yet, the black guards were warriors. We had nearly gutted them but somehow they reformed. They kissed us with iron and threw us back.

Our men wavered. A few streamed past me toward the rear in what quickly threatened to become a rout. As I had feared, our men charged well but had little stomach for the long push. Thus it is sometimes with men who have had their spirit nearly beaten out of them. Yet, I did not think their spirit gone, only hidden. I had to find a way of recharging their courage.

During the fighting I had been forced by the press of men toward the enemy's left flank, where the clans had already been beaten. I saw our attack faltering and raced forward, shouting. My yells went unnoticed against the din. Frantically searching for some way to stem the tide of our retreat, I spotted a tasaber loose among the crowd. I fought my way to him and mounted. He was frightened but I pulled his head around and kicked him in motion toward the Klar center.

Heril, leading a number of Koro and Nokarra, fought a slow retreat in front of the still advancing guards. I called to him. He saw me on the tasaber and rallied his men to me. Around him, other ex-slaves abandoned their retreat and began to move back against the Klar lines. That movement became a run and then a charge, and we hit them solidly and brought their advance to a stop.

For just a moment more the loyalists held, and then the weight of attack on two sides bent their overextended lines inward, bent them further, and snapped them. We surged in, our swords reaping a red harvest, and even the Priests' Guard broke and began to flee. They fled toward Jask's men, toward the Keshaki who hated them almost as much as did the slaves, and they were annihilated.

I brought the tasaber to a halt, and as I dismounted it trembled and collapsed. Only then did I see the arrow that had driven deeply into the barrel of its stomach. As I said before, the tasaber has heart. I would mourn for this one.

Jask came up to me riding a coal black mount. He smiled widely. And why not. He had just won his first battle as a general and it seemed that he would soon be high-council of the Klar, for the back of the Klar resistance had been shattered.

"Except for Nethcormundis," I whispered to myself.

CHAPTER TWENTY-FOUR

NETHCORMUNDIS

Our victorious armies marched on Kwellarn the Lower. Strange to see Klar and those who had once been their slaves pacing along side by side. But then, the Keshaki had much in common with slaves; both had few rights and little power.

There had been only one serious incident between the two forces. An ebon Llurn who had led a squadron of slaves very well during the battle grew quite vocal in his dislike of the Klar. Just as the Keshaki seemed near to responding, I took the fellow aside and explained a few facts to him. He returned to his men with a bloody face but he made no more remarks about our new allies.

With that done, I turned the army of ex-slaves over to Valyan and commandeered a tasaber for a quick ride to Kwellarn. Jask led the way and a few dozen Keshaki and ex-slaves went with us, as did Rannon, who refused to stay behind. Rhandh accompanied his Jhesana, having returned to her side as bodyguard. He held that post alone now, without his Vlih NHa, but I felt she was well looked after.

The tasaber has more endurance than a horse, and despite not leaving the battlefield until late morning the outskirts of Kwellarn hove into view about two dhaur before dusk. I blessed the long Taleran day. The city lay open to us as we approached and the guards at the perimeters bore the insignia-less shields of the Keshaki. These saluted Jask as he rode in, recognizing his blood-red targe.

The city seemed largely intact. Only a few fires smoldered and the streets were remarkably empty of debris.

Bands of Keshaki roved here and there, but we saw few clansmen. Only as we approached the temple quarter did we find fighting still going on. Now I understood why the streets were quiet elsewhere. The majority of the Klar were here.

Our party shoved its way through the crowds, most of whom seemed merely to be observing and awaiting the outcome. Near the gates of the quarter we found Relic, the high priest of the god Heshval, and his forces. These were mainly Keshaki but there were a number of rahnvin fighting slaves among them who also carried weapons. I saw, as well, that more of Heshval's priests and acolytes had joined us than we had hoped. And they were armed.

The high priest seemed not to recognize me at first—well, I had changed a bit—but even after he did notice me he said nothing, only nodded as if to an old acquaintance. His world had changed very suddenly around him and I admired his courage and ability to adapt. Many in his position would not have been able to do so.

Briefly, Relic told us what had happened. His forces had taken the city with little opposition, since the people had grown tired of the Thye Vessoth and most of the clan militias who might have battled them were gone. There had been tough resistance at the temple quarter from the remaining Priests' Guards and from clan forces that had fled inside, and Relic's first two attacks had been repulsed with heavy losses. It had taken him much of the afternoon to prepare his third assault. He did not want this one to fail for fear his troops would lose heart and melt away into the surrounding crowd.

I did not like to think of a frontal assault on the walls with our current forces but there seemed little choice. The slave army and Jask's troops would not reach Kwellarn until late tomorrow and we dared not give the clans time to recover their balance. Too, the greatest sorcerer of the Thye Vessoth waited inside the temple district. From what I'd heard of Nethcormundis he might be able to turn the tide by himself if given enough time.

It seemed our best chance of success lay in splitting the enemy's defense by attacking from several directions at once. The high priest's two failed attempts had focused on a single point, leaving the superbly disciplined Guard with only a limited area to protect. I felt that we had to take advantage of superior numbers to offset the lack of discipline among our own troops.

Jask and Relic agreed with the concept of multiple attacks and it did not take long to divide our forces into three, roughly equal units. Most of the Keshaki went in with the Klar commanders while the majority of the ex-slaves followed me. Archers covered our attack with an arrow storm and our assault carried easily to the wall. There, the blades of friends and enemies alike became very red very fast.

Ladders were thrown up and thrown down just as quickly. Lances and daggers and pottery and rocks showered around us, slicing open wounds or crushing bones and skulls. Our own weapons began to tell and falling bodies joined the rain of other debris. But in the end we were turned back.

We gave our men no time to think of defeat but immediately ordered them forward again. This time Relic and I each sent only sham forces toward our original objectives and mingled the rest of our warriors in with those of Jask. The enemy seemed fooled by the stratagem and we broke through in an area manned by clan militia.

Within minutes the loyalist defense lay in tatters and the enemy was fleeing. We threw open the gates behind them and the remaining rebels surged through. Once inside we lost all control of our forces and they spread out in an orgy of destruction. The masses of onlookers joined in as they realized who the victors would be. Together, the rebels and the mob tried to remove any sign that the Klar/Thye Vessoth alliance had ever existed.

Quite suddenly, the presence of the Thye Vessoth was carried home to us in the worst way. In the center of the temple quarter lay a huge shrine dedicated to Heshval, now desecrated by the image of the snake god while the black statue of the Klar deity had been relegated to a dusty corner full of rubbish. From that direction there roared up a sheet of green flame that burst like flowers in the sky. For the first time on Talera I felt the true power of sorcery. It tingled in my skin and curled my nostrils. The shock wave that followed rattled the knives on my belt.

A rumbling came upon us from the temple shrine and

then a wind howled against us, carrying smoke and cinders. The center of the quarter had disappeared beneath a rising wall of fire. Tasabers screamed and reared. Some broke their tethers and fled. Slaves and Klar alike ceased their rampage and ran as the flames marched along the streets toward us, seemingly eating the stone as they came. I knew this was the work of Nethcormundis and that he would as lief destroy the city as see us take it.

"No," screamed Jask, furious at seeing a victory that was so close about to be snatched from his grasp.

He grabbed for the reins of a nearby tasaber and in a moment was spurring savagely toward the temple and the sorcerer. I shouted to him, then followed on a second tasaber as he failed to heed. I did not think anyone else would come after us, at least not immediately. We had taken the only ta- sabers available, the only ones left except for the old one that Relic rode.

I chased after Jask, seeing him loom out of smoke and then fade into it again an instant later. He rode into a cloud of swirling ash and through walls of flame that reared up on either hand. I reined up, searching, then caught a glimpse of him on the far side still riding for the temple. I urged my own mount through the smoke, both of us choking and our eyes tearing, and when we had broken into the clear again I saw Jask's mount suddenly rear and throw him.

An instant later, my own mount did the same. I hit the ground hard and staggered up, only to find the tasabers flee- ing back the way they had come. I ran over to Jask and helped him to his feet.

"You fool," I shouted in his ear. "What do you think you're doing?"

He looked at me and suddenly laughed. The mad stare that had been on his face only moments before was gone, replaced by something more familiar to me.

"I'm fine," he said. "Come on, let's get out—"

A ponderous tread of feet interrupted him. We glanced up, and saw what had spooked our mounts. The earth around us shook; stones rattled and fell. A shadow loomed out of the pall, coming from the direction of the temple, a shadow fif- teen feet high! The Klar commander gasped, locked for a moment in superstitious awe. I, too, felt it. The statue of Heshval walked out of the smoke and the dust and strode down upon us.

I drew my sword and Jask his. "Well, Ruenn," he said. "Should we run or should we die?"

"Neither. At least not yet. We have to stop that statue. We know it as Thye Vessoth work but if it gets past us your people will take it as a sign of Heshval's disfavor. The revolt will fall apart and all the sacrifices will have been in vain. I cannot allow it."

He grinned at me. "Do you plan to argue the thing out of stepping on us?" he asked.

I grinned back at him and for the first time in a long while felt the emotion go deeper than my face.

"Don't worry. You're too ugly to squish. Come on, let's topple this thing."

The monster saw us as we sprinted out of the twisting smoke toward it, bending its head down at us with torches flaring in its dark sockets. Perhaps "saw" was wrong, for the thing could not see with the fires it wore for eyes, but the malevolence behind those eyes sensed us and turned the thing lose to raven us. It moved more swiftly than I could have imagined, coming down with a black stone foot nearly three feet long in an effort to smash us under.

I vaulted aside and struck with the edge of my sword. The hard steel shattered on the hard stone. I heard Jask shout, "Aiee!" and then the strike of his own blade. The steel rang and splintered, and Jask slipped to his knees. Heshval stomped down at him. He rolled away. The statue stomped again, and again the Keshaki rolled, barely escaping.

I threw a rock at the god's back and bellowed at it. It turned. Its eyes blazed and it came for me. I ran into a pall of smoke thrown off by a burning building. Heshval followed. Jask was nowhere to be seen.

I threw another stone, then backpedaled rapidly. The thing followed and I kept just ahead of it, not allowing it to lose sight of me. If it did, then it would turn back into the main streets. And if it came upon our forces in those narrow thoroughfares it would wreak red havoc.

Desperately, my mind groped for some way to stop the

monster. Steel seemed to have little effect. Then Jask came out of the dust behind the statue and hurled himself at its legs. The thing staggered but the Klar's weight was too inconsequential to do more. It gave me an idea, though.

As Heshval turned on Jask, I picked up a piece of fallen lumber and whacked it behind the legs. The wood broke but I had its attention and it turned again toward me. I ran away, right into a blowing wall of smoke. It came on, and I spun about while hidden in the smudge and ran back at it. It reached for me and I somersaulted between its legs, almost colliding with Jask coming from the other direction. It took the monster just a moment to arrest its forward momentum.

"Together," I shouted at Jask.

He nodded and we rushed forward and hurled ourselves into the backs of Heshval's knees. Again the idol staggered. We moved quicker than it could right itself and leaped in a second time. It swayed.

Jask grabbed up a block of fallen masonry and smashed it into the giant's ankle. I joined him, using a length of iron from a ruined doorway. Heshval swatted at me and missed, and when it tried to take a step Jask and I threw our weight against the lifting foot simultaneously.

The thing lost its balance and the huge foot came down on a piece of rubble that slid beneath it. We ran for our lives. The monster reeled, and then was falling. It crashed against a massive wall of red lava blocks, bringing the whole structure down on its head. In an instant the statue disappeared beneath tons of collapsing rock. I flashed Jask a smile and we turned as one and sprinted back through the smoke toward the shrine of Heshval, toward Nethcormundis.

It did not take long to reach the temple. It had once been more magnificent and sumptuous than the temple in Kwellarn the Upper. Now, in the quickly dimming light of the Andertalen evening, it was half rubble, with two of its walls blasted down by some tremendous explosion. We rushed up the cracked steps side by side, Jask the Klar and Ruenn the ex-slave. A dead warrior of the Priests' Guard lay at the temple portal and I slowed to wrest a fallen sword from his stiff fingers. Thus it was that Jask went in a step ahead of me. I heard him yell and raced after.

As I entered I saw a Thye Vessoth—Nethcormundis I knew—at the foot of the altar, the ophidian head of his odious god in stone relief behind him. He was standing, though Rannon had said he was crippled and I could see the braces of metal on his legs and back. He was standing, and in his hand glittered an odd, milk-white stone. It was a toir'in-or, not a wand but the real thing, and it ached with brilliance. The envelope of the stone's power surrounded the wizard, giving him the strength to rise on bent legs, giving him the strength to kill.

It was not Nethcormundis, however, that had rung the shout from Jask's lips. A shadow as insubstantial as mist dived on him in a rushing wind. It struck him and he staggered back, crying out again, this time in pain. Two red coals, like eyes, winked in the midst of the shadow before it swooped up into the cavernous vault of the temple to be lost amid other darknesses. I grabbed Jask's shoulder and jerked my hand back as it burned with intense cold. The Klar warrior collapsed at my feet, unconscious.

I looked at Nethcormundis. His body seemed swollen with venom and the bat-wing vanes at the sides of his head stood out rigidly. I ran forward. Shadows coalesced above me and swept down. I dived for the floor at the last minute and felt the icy breath of a thousand winters pass inches above me. I hit and rolled and came up running.

Something like an emerald wasp of vast size rose out of the floor. It arched its tail and I sworded it through the abdomen. The blade met only a faint resistance before the image burst like a swamp bubble, leaving behind a foul stench. I ran on, thinking only of the sorcerer.

A wall wavered into existence before me but I was moving so swiftly that I burst through before it could harden. For an instant it felt like I was struggling through mud and then I came free. And a stone head snapped into being in front of me. It screamed, vomiting a stream of lava that splashed on the floor where I had been. I was already past it and at the foot of the altar.

I saw the Thye Vessoth's face then, felt its gaze focus power upon me, felt that power crushing down. My legs slowed. Without my will. The sword dragged at my hand, turning to lead. I saw the appendages at the side of the beast's head fill with a milky gleam, saw its blue, blue eyes, so clear and yet so intoxicated. Nethcormundis was drunk on the energy of the toir'in-or, and he was going insane.

That insanity could destroy us all.

A monstrous serpent formed over my head, wearing the visage of Vessoth. It coiled its neck and opened a red mouth to strike. It was real enough to kill me. But strain as I might, I could not move. Then a voice called out. I heard what it said.

"No!" Rannon shouted. "No, my love!"

The world had turned to amber around me but somehow I twisted my head just enough to see her. She stood at the temple's door, a sword and dagger in her hands, the last light of the day limning her slender form. Nethcormundis lifted his eyes and reached out to swat her.

The arm that the beast extended carried the toir'in-or and glowed alabaster for its entire length. I knew the lizard-priest would kill my woman before he killed me. But he had lifted his eyes. His hold on me weakened, as a drunk will let something fall from his grip without awareness, and the thought of Rannon dying stabbed such a flame of rage through me that the stillness around me shattered.

Even as an explosion formed at the tip of Nethcormundis's fingers, I lunged forward and drove my blade deep into his chest, slicing easily through the envelope of light that surrounded him. Once again, as it had on Earth, steel interfered with the magic of the stone.

Nethcormundis stood whole for only an instant, his eyes wide, the sword in his body. Then there came a crack as of glass breaking and holes opened in the sorcerer's flesh, white holes that hungered and tore at him. He screamed once and collapsed to his knees, his flesh bubbling and stinking, bones fracturing audibly in his limbs.

The sword hilt became red-hot and I let go as Nethcormundis fell onto his face and lay still. Over his shoulder, the image of the giant snake just...went away. The toir'in-or rolled from the priest's fingers, striking the stone flaggings with a dull clunk. Outside in the city, the flames nurtured by sorcery began to wane.

I turned and caught Rannon in my arms as she ran through the rubble to me. Her face was tear-stained and covered with soot. Yet, she was lovely. I kissed her once, but it lasted long. We stopped only as the thought of Jask struck through us both at the same time. He was alive and stirring when we reached him. He came fully awake all of a sudden and sat up under my hands.

"Nethcormundis?" he asked.

"Dead," I said, then grinned at him. "While you napped here on the floor."

He looked up at me and shook his head. "You kill him?"

"Yeah, with a little help from Rannon."

He glanced from one to the other of us. "I am grateful," he said.

I pulled him to his feet. He winced as his weight came down on his left leg. "By Hesh—I mean by—Oh well, by whatever. That shadow thing nearly froze me to the marrow. My leg still feels numb."

"I'm sure the feeling will come back," I said. "Sometime."

"You're reassuring," he grumbled. Then he pulled away from my arm and walked down the darkened temple aisle toward the altar.

We came up beside him as he stood looking down at the partially melted corpse of Nethcormundis. Only then did I think of the questions that I had intended to ask the Thye Vessoth about Bryce and others of my old crew from Earth. There had been no chance, but I did not regret the wizard's death.

Jask reached out with a booted foot and touched the rapidly cooling milkstone. "So, it is over," he said.

"Yes," I agreed.

But this was Talera and it was not quite over.

CHAPTER TWENTY-FIVE

HUNTERS FROM THE SKY

I barely had time to agree with Jask that it was over before we heard the sound of hooves storming up outside. It was, as I expected, Rhandh and a number of our men. Many carried torches, for night had fallen.

After Jask and I had ridden for the temple, Rannon had taken the only available tasaber, that of Relic, and come after us. She had been the last to get through the fire, though the old beast she rode collapsed halfway to the shrine. Rhandh had tried to follow her on foot but had been stymied by the flames.

Other tasabers had been brought, but only after Nethcormundis's death and the waning of the fires could our people make their way through to us. The Vlih was quite wroth with Rannon, rightly so, and she apologized meekly enough to sooth him. It was just a little bit amusing but I did not dare laugh.

With Rhandh had come a number of Klar, including a youth who we had not seen before. His face frowned anxiously and my blood ran cold.

Jask sensed something wrong at the same time. "What is it?" he demanded of the young Keshaki. "What's wrong?"

"My lord," the lad said. "The upper city. It is attacked."

"By who," Jask demanded.

"I do not know," the messenger said, "but they struck out of the sky aboard flying ships."

Jask proved then that he was fit to lead. The pain in his legs was instantly forgotten as a new threat loomed up. His orders rattled out and couriers rushed to fulfill them.

He turned to us. "I thank you my friends but your fight is over. It is the Klar now who must defend our gains."

"Don't be an idiot," I said. "I can't command any of the others to accompany you but I'll be going."

"And I," said Rannon.

"And I," snapped Rhandh.

"And we," shouted a dozen warriors who had once been slaves, their swords leaping out in salute.

"Then we must hurry," Jask said. "I have sent word to Relic and the rest of our forces to follow me to the surface. I must go at once myself to see what may be done."

None of us spoke. There was no need. We ran to the tasabers, mounted, and tore out of the temple district toward the long slope leading up to the outer world. Our mounts covered the short distance rapidly. The bronze gates to Talen stood open and there were no guards. We stormed through them, and down the temple aisle, and out the doors into Kwellarn the Upper.

The tasabers took the temple steps with liquid grace and we were free once more under the sky of Talera. Though night had cloaked Andertalen, it was only mid-afternoon here, for the nights and days above and below are not synchronized. Here the sun shone, and had turned crimson.

Then diving shapes hissed out of the blood-red sky. Above them drifted other forms, giant shadows that floated majestically over. From these rained a hail of small objects that bloomed in fire when they struck the ground.

I gasped as I realized that the large shadows were ships, not airplanes but true ships of the sky.[4] Their hulls were of

---

[4]Only later did I learn how the sky ships of Talera are driven. Crystals charged by the toir'in-or are used to provide lift in the larger ships while sails provide the primary motive force. Toir'in-or are, of course, capable of powering the largest of vessels but are too rare for such use. Charged wands are attached to rotors in the smaller ships to provide both lift and drive, and wings and flaps help stabilize the lighter craft.

A caste of flyers exists on Talera who have been trained from birth to use the stones and wands for powering air boats. These are not sorcerers for the most part and can only use the stones for the one purpose. They are also respected and protected. To injure a flyer except in air combat is punishable by death.—Ruenn Maclang.

wood, and decks rose up above with masts and billowing sails that glittered in the high sun. They were the size of battleships but floated as gracefully as feathers. The dark flitting forms that swept below them were also ships, only smaller and without sails. Yet, I heard no drone of engines.

Even as we watched, the fire-rain ceased and the smaller craft dived down to land, disgorging strike forces of soldiers for the next stage of the assault. There seemed little organized resistance from the slavers. Frantically, Jask screamed out orders and the Klar with us ran to obey.

And then I heard Rannon's voice. I was watching Kwellarn burn and her words scarcely registered at first. When they did the shock staggered me.

"It is my father's fleet," she said.

Her father's fleet! I had concluded from the way Rhandh acted toward her that Rannon was someone of importance, the daughter of a wealthy merchant perhaps, or even a noble. But surely no merchant or noble could have raised a fleet such as that which soared over Kwellarn. No less than an emperor could have done so.

Did that mean that Rannon—my Rannon—was a princess? It did not seem possible. She was certainly beautiful enough, but I had always considered princesses to be a rather dainty bunch. Admittedly, I had never met one. But I had always pictured them as frail morning flowers who would wilt in the heat of midday. Rannon was not frail, and she thrived in the heat as her time in the lava mines had shown. I shook my head.

Rannon's next words deepened my shock. There seemed a new something in her voice, a sense of command, or perhaps my imagination provided the change.

She turned to Jask and I. "I must get to one of the landing ships," she said. "I think I can get the attack stopped."

Jask started forward immediately on his tasaber, searching his way through the turmoil of the streets toward the place where a troop carrier had touched down. We followed, smoke wafting in clouds over us. We had to force our way through streams of refugees headed toward Andertalen, but at last we broke through the smoke to find one of the invading airships before us.

The Taleran equivalent of marines had already thrown up a defensive perimeter around the vessel and heavier weapons, trebuchets and scorpions, were being unloaded. We raced up to them with Rannon and I in the front and the Klar behind. They saw us coming and formed a double line, pikemen at the fore and archers behind. Arrows were nocked but Rannon called out in a high voice, in a tongue that I did not recognize, and an officer of the bowmen snapped up his arm to stay his men's hands.

Rannon dismounted and walked forward, Jask, Rhandh, and I backing her up. The officer came to meet us, and when he saw Rannon his eyes widened and he suddenly dipped to one knee.

"Jhesana," he said. I translated it now as princess. "Thank Severian you are safe."

"There is not time for thanks, Captain," Rannon said, rushing her words. "You must take us at once to my father's ship. He is here, is he not?"

The Captain stammered a bit. "Yes. Yes, of course, Jhesana. Your father, the Emperor, is here, but...."

"There is no time for buts either, Captain. Take us at once. And order your attacks to cease immediately."

Still he hesitated.

"Move, man," Rannon said, exasperated, "while there's still something left to save."

He moved at that.

The four of us were hustled aboard the troop carrier and it leaped quickly into the sky. I still heard no engines, but in only a moment we were high above the city, speeding toward a giant of a ship with a maroon and gray flag at its mast. The vessel itself was painted gray, and on the bottom of the hull, in maroon, was drawn the image of a raptor. This was, I learned, the trenkil, which resembles an eagle except that it is bigger and much more vicious.

As we neared the larger craft I saw that a golden border surrounded its flag, a king's mark perhaps, and many smaller flags were being waved on the deck. These seemed to be signals, some apparently meant for us. Flags flashed from our own deck, answering in the proper tongue, and our Captain brought us alongside with ease.

The ships were roped together and a gangplank laid out across the decks. Rannon dashed across this as if she were not a thousand feet in the air. Jask followed, seemingly unconcerned. I swallowed hard and raced across behind them, not looking down.

Marines on the deck watched us with steel eyes and hard hands. They looked competent and disciplined, but when they saw Rannon they all quickly dropped to one knee. She only nodded at them and went past.

Around the corner of a deck cabin came several men who did not drop to a knee. Their leader was a heavily muscled warrior dressed in silver armor and a maroon cape. A winged helmet sat above his dark hair and hawk-like visage. He and Rannon resembled each other, I noted, mainly in the hair and in the eyes. His irises, too, gleamed a vivid blue. So, this must be Rannon's father and the commander of this mighty air fleet.

Rannon rushed forward to him but did not at first throw herself into his arms. He looked at her, then tossed aside the sword and shield he carried and crushed her to his chest. The others who had accompanied the Emperor also crowded around, nobles by the look of them, though one with light colored eyes looked enough like Rannon to be her kinsman. Only for a moment did the Emperor hold his daughter, then he pushed her back and looked beyond her shoulder at Jask and I.

"What—?" he started to ask, but Rannon stopped him with a hand to his chest.

"You must end your attack on the city at once, Father," she said.

He glanced at her, then back to us. I noted that he looked mainly at Jask, and there seemed little friendship in his eyes.

"Tell me why, Daughter. The Klar must be punished for this."

"But you're punishing the wrong Klar," she said.

She turned and pointed at Jask. "This man." She called him man though he was not. "He saved us all, including me. And he has led a rebellion against the former leaders of the slavers. He has freed the slaves. You must stop the attack or you will undo all the good he has accomplished."

193

Rannon's father was an Emperor as I had imagined one to be. He considered swiftly, then snapped out commands, his voice arrogant. Warriors leaped to obey. Flags were run up the masts and horns sounded. The fighting below ceased almost immediately, and the ships that had landed began to lift skyward again with their compliment of troops aboard. Then the Emperor strode over to Jask and I, his nobles at his heels.

"I am Hurnan Jystral," he said, "Emperor of Nyshphal. This," he waved to the fellow who resembled Rannon, "is my son, Kuurus."

He then directed his words at Jask. "What is your name, Klar?"

"I am Jask," the one-time pirate said, "High-Council of the Klar. We do not wish war with Nyshphal," he added.

"If what my daughter says is the truth then you will not have it."

"It is true," I said.

"Who are you?" he asked, looking directly into my eyes.

"Ruenn Maclang."

"And what part did you play in this?"

"Only that of a soldier," I said.

"That is not exactly true, Father," Rannon said. "He saved my life as well as defended my honor. And he led the slaves in a revolt that played a major role in the Klar rebellion."

The Emperor's eyes did not leave mine. "I thank you for my daughter's life," he said.

I inclined my head in acknowledgement.

Finally, he looked away. "Well," he said to Jask, "it seems that I owe you and your people an apology. We will, of course, pay reparations for the damage."

"You owe us nothing," Jask said. "Klar helped take your daughter, and you could not know that a rebellion had been fought here and won. However, I would ask how you knew Rannon was among us? And how you found us?"

Jystral nodded. "Kuurus," he ordered, "go fetch our prisoner."

The prince left but returned only moments later, guards behind him dragging a bound Human. I recognized the man, though he did not look quite the dandy that he had the last time we met. Because of him I had once been whipped.

"Durhain!" Rannon exclaimed. "How did you get here?"

The slim noble looked up once and quickly lowered his gaze again. "Forgive me, Jhesana," he said. He fell to his knees before her. "I beg you to forgive me." His eyes filled with tears.

Rannon looked down on the man who had been responsible for all her misery. Her gaze grew suddenly angry, then cold. Then she softened.

"I cannot understand your actions, Durhain. But I forgive you."

"Thank you, Jhesana," the noble said, his voice broken and aching. He did not now seem proud and arrogant.

"How did you come to be my father's prisoner?" Rannon asked him.

"His men found me, Jhesana. When...when I had served my usefulness to the Klar they ordered me set adrift on the sea with no food or drink. They thought I would die. But I was lucky. I got caught in an ocean current and there were many days of rain. Finally, I washed up on an island and lived there for a time until one of your father's, the Emperor's, ships found me while searching for you. I told them my story and your father gathered his fleet and came here. He brought me along to show the way and to be punished at your whim."

Durhain looked up at Rannon, so tall over him. In his eyes glistened more tears, like those of a child. "Punish me if you wish, Jhesana. I deserve no better."

"Choose a punishment, Daughter," the Emperor said, "and it will be carried out."

Rannon looked from Durhain to her father, and, inexplicably I thought, to me. I said nothing.

She turned her eyes back to her father. "I think he has been punished enough," she said.

The Emperor gazed long at her, then sighed as if resigned to his daughter's softness. "Very well. Since you wish it, I will not have him killed. However, neither will I have such scum in my empire. Let him rot in exile."

Durhain shivered but made no response. Nor did

Rannon speak, realizing that her father's mind was made up.

Hurnan Jystral then turned to Jask, the new High-Council of the Klar. "We must speak of the future," he said. "Perhaps you and your council will accept my invitation to a feast. Given," he turned to Rannon, "in honor of my daughter."

Jask drew up his shoulders. "I should be happy to accept, Emperor, but there remains much to be done in my land. If you will return me to the surface I must see to gaining control over the fires and consolidating the revolution."

"Of course," Jystral said. "I respect your wishes and offer you my aid and that of my fleet."

"We will accept it," Jask said. "Then there will be a time for feasting."

CHAPTER TWENTY-SIX

THE LAST BATTLE

It was autumn on Talera but still warm in the far south of the planet where lay the Klar homeland. We were aloft in the sky-battleship of Hurnan Jystral, Emperor of Nyshphal and father of Rannon. It was night and the winds blew soft about us, sighing in the rigging where lights were strung for the festival.

Many days had passed since Jystral's arrival at Talen. Much had been accomplished. Jask's hold on power had been consolidated and a new council representing all of the Klar had been chosen. The slaves had been given their freedom and the majority of them would sail back to Nyshphal with the air fleet to wend their long way home from there. The injured, the lame, and the blind, had been invited by Jedik's people to join them in Emira and many had accepted.

Vriun was appointed a court physician by Rannon and would go to Nyshphal. Rhandh, too, would return to Nyshphal, there to serve as bodyguard for his Jhesana. I was happy for that. I had scarcely seen Valyan or Heril and did not know their plans. Nor was I sure of my own. Bryce was still out there somewhere, but with Nethcormundis and his Thye Vessoth dead I had no idea where to search.

I leaned over the railing of the wind-ship and watched the black sea far below. In it lay the island of Talen, starred by lights. The deck beneath my feet thrummed with music. The feast was well underway, with much dancing and singing, and games were played on the deck and elsewhere. Wine and ale had flowed freely and food had been consumed in huge quantities. I had done little of it.

Now that I had time to think, now that every minute was not taken up with the fight to survive, I suddenly realized that I was alone in a way few others on Talera could ever be. There were no other people of Earth here with me, and no place on this planet where I belonged. I suppose I was feeling a bit sorry for myself and had left the feast below and come up on the cooler deck.

Too, other thoughts crowded in my mind, other reasons for fleeing the festivities. I could no longer bear the sight of the most beautiful girl in the world—in two worlds—Rannon, who was a princess and out of my reach. I heard a sound then and turned, expecting some drunken reveler, but my very thoughts stood there, dressed in white silk. She was lovely.

"So here you are, Ruenn," she said. "I wondered where you had gone."

"Only to get a breath of fresh air, my lady," I said.

She smiled. "You need not call me my lady, Ruenn. We have been through too much to insist on formalities."

"Yes, of course, Rannon," I said, forcing a smile.

She walked to stand beside me at the rail. She too looked down at Talen and its sparkling lights. Then, as if reaching a decision, she turned to me.

"What are your plans now?" she asked. "If you do not mind my question."

"I do not mind the question but I do not really know the answer," I said. "I know that I must continue the search for my brother."

"You could continue that search from Nyshphal," she said.

I looked at her curiously.

"I mean," she said, rushing on with her words, "Nyshphal vessels trade over great stretches of the sea and our air fleets travel the skies. We could send word with them. Would it not be better to have many people searching for your brother instead of only one?"

I had to admit that it was.

"Then you will come to Nyshphal?"

"I do not know, my lady. I do not know. I must...."

198

"I see," she said, and turned abruptly to go.

I grabbed her arm. "Wait," I said.

"Why should I?" she snapped, anger flaring in her voice. "Why should I when it is obvious that you wish to be alone. You do not want me here. You have made that perfectly clear by ignoring me for the past few weeks. I had thought us friends."

"I did not mean to ignore you," I said.

"Do not lie to me," she said. "At least do not do that."

I looked down from her eyes, knowing that she spoke the truth.

"Why did you not tell me that your father was an Emperor?" I asked at last.

"Would that have changed the way you acted toward me?"

"It might have," I said.

"That is what I thought you would say."

I still held her arm and now she tried to pull away. I looked again at her and did not release my grip.

"Let go of me please," she said.

"No," I said.

Her eyes blazed up. "You will do as I command!"

"No," I said, and pulled her into my arms. She did not struggle but turned her lips up to mine. They were sweet and yielding and I kissed her fiercely. Abruptly, it seemed that the night had grown much warmer. After a bit she drew back. I let her go, reluctantly.

A smile curved her face. "You dare much, warrior."

"I love you," I said.

"And I love you."

I reached to touch her hair and we would have kissed again, but light suddenly flooded the planks and Valyan, Heril, Kreeg the ex-gladiator and a dozen others that I knew burst forth onto the deck. They sang and toasted each other in loud voices, but stopped when they saw Rannon, suddenly subdued. She laughed and snatched a wine bottle from Valyan's hand and guzzled a swig. She handed it to me and I took my own gulp. Her hand slipped into mine and I laughed at something Heril said. I have no idea what it was.

We drank long that night and I remember Valyan and

Heril saying that they would accompany me wherever I went, and they reminded me that they had both offered me their loyalty once before on the side of a mountain in Emira. In honor, I could do no less than accept it. I was much surprised that Kreeg, too, swore his loyalty to me. I took his hand on it.

In the pink dawn the warship of the Emperor of Nyshphal turned its raptor prow toward its home island, and I was aboard with the woman I loved and many friends.

CHAPTER TWENTY-SEVEN

A SONG OF ENDINGS

I put down the quill pen, and stood up, and went to the window. It was dawn. The winter sun was rising, blue-white, casting a sheen beautifully on the snow, and I had been writing through much of the night so that the record of my first months on Talera would be complete.

Outside the window lay the rocky ground of northern Nyshphal and the rich darkness of a wild forest. Morning glistened from the white powder of the snow and from the icicles that hung like crystal teeth under the eaves of Hurnan Jystral's hunting lodge, and from the steel gray peaks that rose above the valley where the cabin stood.

Talera was my world now, and it was lovely. Yet, I would leave it today. If only for a short time. I had to return to Earth. Throughout my first weeks on Talera I had longed to return home and had known of no way to do so. Now I knew of a way but did not wish to go.

There was a sphere gate on Nyshphal, only a few hundred yards from where I stood. And there were those here who knew how to work its magic, though they warned me that much may have changed on Earth. They say that because of the way I came to Talera, through the destruction of a toir'in-or, that time may have been distorted and that I am likely to end up sometime in the future of my own world. Yet, I must make the journey. If I can, I would ease the pain of my parents, who have lost their sons. And if they are gone then there are my sisters and their descendents to see to.

But I would return to Talera. Bryce and my cousin Eric

were still lost here somewhere. And there was Rannon, my Rannon. I had said my goodbyes to her yesterday before flying up here to be near the sphere gate. She had not wanted me to leave but had understood my need to go. But I would be back. They had told me, those who knew the ways of the toir'in-or gates, that I had sixty days to complete my work on Earth and return to the place where I first appeared. At that time they would open the gate and I would be drawn through. If I were there. I would be, I vowed.

Now it was almost time for the sphere gate to be opened here. I turned to leave, stopping only long enough to pick up the manuscript and to sheath a dagger at my hip. As well, I gathered two leather pouches, one filled with jewels, the other with gold. I would have need of money on Earth. I stroked once the hilt of the sword that I would leave behind and strode out the door.

ABOUT THE AUTHOR

CHARLES ALLEN GRAMLICH grew up on a farm in Arkan-
sas, near the foothills of the Ozark Mountains, then moved to
the New Orleans area in 1986. He's since sold several novels
and numerous short stories. His tales, while mostly in the
genres of horror, science fiction, and fantasy, have also included westerns, children's stories, mainstream fiction, slip-
stream works, and experimental pieces. He has also pub-
lished poetry and nonfiction, the latter ranging from refer-
ence works to articles on writing. He refuses to comment,
however, on rumors that most of his work is actually written
by Ruenn Maclang.

Charles is a member of REHupa (the Robert E. Howard
United Press Association), HWA (the Horror Writers Asso-
ciation), and SFPA (the Science Fiction Poetry Association).
He produces a regular column on writing for *The Illuminata*,
an online magazine, and is the horror moderator at United
Sci Fi Forums. His blog can be found at:

Http://charlesgramlich.blogspot.com

www.ingramcontent.com/pod-product-compliance
Lightning Source LLC
Chambersburg PA
CBHW032006240626
47153CB00003B/1136